UNINVITED

AMANDA MARRONE

More thrilling reads from Simon Pulse

Tripping to Somewhere
Kristopher Reisz

Tithe
and
Valiant
Holly Black

The Uglies series
Scott Westerfeld

The Seven Deadly Sins series
Robin Wasserman

UNINVITED

AMANDA MARRONE

Simon Pulse

New York   London   Toronto   Sydney

This book is a work of fiction. Any references to historical events, real people, or real locales are used fictitiously. Other names, characters, places, and incidents are the product of the author's imagination, and any resemblance to actual events or locales or persons, living or dead, is entirely coincidental.

SIMON PULSE
An imprint of Simon & Schuster Children's Publishing Division
1230 Avenue of the Americas, New York, NY 10020
Copyright © 2007 by Amanda Marrone
All rights reserved, including the right of reproduction in
whole or in part in any form.
SIMON PULSE and colophon are registered trademarks
of Simon & Schuster, Inc.
Designed by Greg Stadnyk and Tom Daly
The text of this book was set in Arrus BT.
Manufactured in the United States of America
First Simon Pulse edition October 2007
10 9 8 7
Library of Congress Control Number 2007925721
ISBN-13: 978-1-4169-3978-8
ISBN-10: 1-4169-3978-4

Dedicated to the memory
of Kathleen Burns Hart—we miss you

ACKNOWLEDGMENTS

There are so many people I want to thank. Those who were there in the beginning—Scottie Robinson, Donna Capern, Toni Buzzeo, Jeanne Munn Bracken, all the Loonies, and especially Patty Schremmer, who was instrumental in helping me figure out this writing stuff. More recently I want to thank my wonderful critique group—Nina Nelson, Pam Foard, Naomi Panzer, and Rob Walsh for reading numerous drafts, giving feedback, and endless encouragement—also Missy Hatch; Rich DiCarlo; Nancy White Cassidy; and Jean.

Many thanks to Nadia Cornier, Jen Weiss Handler, Lauren Barnholdt, and everyone at Simon Pulse for believing in me; and to my fabulous editor, Jen Klonsky, for adopting the story and whose wonderful suggestions made this into a much better book. Thank you, Barry Goldblatt, for coming up with the title. Thanks to Janine Klein (my first target-audience reader), NESCBWI, all my Live Journal friends, and everyone at Verla Kay's for cheering me on, especially Kelsey Johnson Defatte, who was always available for a quick read and wonderful advice; Cindy Rosen Ramsey, for sharing her imagination with me when we were kids; my husband, Joe, without whom this book couldn't have happened; my mother, Marilou Foley, for all her support; and lastly my father, Jerry Malloy, for telling me scary stories, taking me to the graveyard, and making me knock on mausoleum doors. I hold him directly responsible for anything dark and twisted in this book.

CHAPTER ONE

I close my eyes, hoping he won't come tonight. It's later than usual. I hope he's given up, or just gone, and I can finally sleep. Cool air blows through the window, and I marvel at my bravery. Or stupidity. It's opened just a crack, no more than an inch. But until tonight I've kept it closed, so I know he'll be wondering what it means.

I listen for some movement in the branches outside, but the leaves are dry and noisy now. I open my eyes— I have to look. It's better when I see him coming. I put every ounce of energy into listening, waiting for my eyes to adjust to the dark. I turn my head, grimacing at the sound of my long hair against the pillowcase. I look out my window, searching the branches, wondering if he'd still come if I chopped down the tree.

"Jordan, are you awake?"

My heart races as I hunt for Michael among the branches. His dark form is pressed against the trunk a few feet higher from his usual perch. How long has he been watching me? He drops down, settling in closer to the window, and I remind myself to look for an ax in the morning.

"Jordan, let me in."

"Go away, Michael. I will never let you in." My voice is steady and calm, without emotion. I've said these words a hundred times today, so they'd become automatic. So I wouldn't change my mind.

Michael sighs, and I think I see him nodding. He knows I'm not ready to let him in. I suspect he knows I think about it, though. I suspect he knows that a part of me wants to.

"You don't know how good you have it, Jo."

I don't like where this is leading. This won't be a "let's talk about the future" night. Michael's missing his old life and he'll keep me up for hours if I encourage him.

"Did you go to school today? Did anyone talk about me?"

I roll my eyes. "This is high school, Michael, you're old news. People have found better things to gossip about. I mean, dying in the summer . . . well, your timing was way off. If having people remember you is important, that is. There's just way too much happening, people move on pretty quickly. Now, if you had died during the school year, that would have made a bigger impact."

"God, Jo! This isn't easy for me, you know."

I nod and wonder if his eyes see better than mine. Can he see I'm putting on an act, that every inch of my skin tingles when he sits outside my window? "I'm sorry, Michael, but I'm tired. I need to sleep."

"But I miss you, Jo. It's not like you think. I can't sleep. I can't sleep at all. I'm awake with nothing to do. Nothing to do but think, and miss you."

"I'll leave some books outside for you tomorrow. Maybe you can accomplish something you never did when you were alive—you can actually read a book. Or, hey, how about this? You can walk into the sunlight and end this all. Have you thought of that? What would happen if you walked into the sun?"

Michael's quiet, and I think he may keep it short tonight—until he taps his foot on my window.

"How's Steve and Eric?" he asks. "They still playing ball?"

"Oh God." I turn my back to the window. "Ask me something I care about. Your stupid friends are exactly the same as they were when you were alive. They live and breathe football or basketball or whatever stupid ball season it is. They still hang out with their gorgeous girlfriends and they still smash mailboxes after a few too many beers. I'm surprised you haven't joined them. That was one of your favorite pastimes, wasn't it?"

He doesn't answer, and I remember Michael making out with some girl—one hand up her short skirt, pressing her against the lockers—acting like he wasn't making an ass of himself. I wonder how many guys walking past dreamed of trading places with Michael? I know how often I dreamed of trading places with that girl.

"So, what, they don't talk about me? Like, not at all?"

He's definitely not letting it go tonight. I think he actually thought they'd worship him forever.

I turn back to the window, but I remember to move slowly this time. I've seen my cat throw itself against the window trying to catch the birds outside in the tree. I sometimes wonder if Michael will lose patience with me and begin to think of me like that, like a bird. Like his prey. So I move bit by bit because I don't know what I would do if Michael were to throw himself against the glass.

"I lied before," I finally say. "Everyone talks about you. They actually talk about you a lot." I pause and let Michael think what he will. "But they're not reminiscing. They think you killed yourself." I've wanted to tell Michael this for a long time, but he was such a mess over the summer, it didn't seem right. But tonight I'm feeling mean, and I won't baby him. Besides, he doesn't seem to care about what his visits do to me.

"What? Who thinks that?"

"Everyone. Everyone at school. And I've been wondering, too." I bite my lip, deciding if I should go on.

"I've told you what happened," he says sharply. "You know what I was dealing with. There's no way I could have stopped it."

I've been wondering if that's true, but I can't tell him that—not yet. "Well, they think you killed yourself and they talk about why you did it. And not just your friends. Everyone."

I let my words sink in. I let him mull over the thought of the entire school ignoring his football record in favor of gossip.

"You wouldn't believe the theories that went around. Some were really laughable. 'Michael was bipolar.' 'Michael only had one month to live.' But don't feel too bad, it was purely defensive. People needed to find the flaws they'd missed when you were alive, because if the great Michael Green couldn't handle things, how is everybody else supposed to?"

"Well, at least you know the truth," he says.

I've wounded him and catch myself before a satisfied smile emerges on my face. I'm long past trying to understand what Michael does to me. Making me wish he were here in my room—in my bed—again, then the next minute making me relish the hurt in his voice. But I won't beat myself up for bruising his ego. He's made me his prisoner every night, and I'm glad when I can get a dig in.

"Damn it!" he growls, startling me. "I'm sick of talking. Let me in!"

He suddenly shifts his weight and slaps his palms against the glass. I flinch like it's me he's hit. I try to shrink away from him and sink into the mattress. God, why did I say those things?

My mouth dries to paper as I suck in the cold

air pouring in over the sill. I make myself as small as possible and freeze into place. So far the window has barred his way. But that damn inch. I imagine him with new cat eyes that can see in the dark, noticing the currents of air playing around the opening. Does he know what I did—can he see? Is that small opening invitation enough for him to enter?

"Jordan," he croons. "I'm sorry. I'm so sorry. I didn't mean to scare you. I just miss you so much. I just want to be with you."

He jumps down to the ground, and I melt into the bed.

I'm shaking, but I won't pull up the blanket. I need to feel the cold; I need to feel something besides the ache I get when he leaves me. I hate myself for wanting him, for feeling flattered it's me he haunts every night.

Three months now I've talked to him through the window. Three months I've conjured his face from the time when he was mine. I see his chestnut eyes, his brown curls, his white, white teeth, and full mouth. I put that face on over the shadows and imagine we could start over.

But the leaves are falling and soon Michael will sit on bare branches. Moonlight will finally find its way to his face, and I'll see what I know is true: that Michael is a monster.

I'm just afraid that one of these nights I might let him in.

CHAPTER TWO

On the way to school this morning, Rachael asked me if I've always been a head case, or if it was more of a gradual loss of sanity. It was a good question, really. It got me thinking. I mean why *would* a person of sound mind sit back and let Michael Green hold her hostage every night? Shouldn't I have come up with some sort of plan to get rid of him by now? And, above all, why did someone like me get involved with Michael in the first place?

Of course, Rachael wasn't referring to my nightly confabs with Michael. As far as she's concerned, Michael Green's dead and buried and, as she was already questioning my sanity, I thought it best to keep my mouth shut.

I laughed off her *"Why the hell are you so scared to pick up the phone and call me, or, more importantly, Danny?"* question, hoping she'd drop it, even though I knew better. Ever since she took Mr. Bell's psych class last semester, it's been her mission in life to point out all of our supposed issues, and offer helpful suggestions for improvement. She doesn't seem to realize that taking one psych class and spending the summer in the self-help section in the bookstore doesn't qualify her to examine the crap out of everyone.

And why should she care if I blew things with Danny because I was too scared to call him back?

Lisa understood my phone phobia thing. Lisa didn't get bent out of shape if I didn't call. Not that Lisa calls me anymore, but at least when we were friends she'd just make a list of things I could do to deal with my anxiety and consider her part done.

I wonder what kinds of lists Lisa is making in rehab.

I wonder if I could call Lisa. I want to tell her what a mess everything is. That I go to school hungover, that I wish I was there with her because I've lost control of my life, and isn't that what rehab is for? To recapture your control?

I mean, never mind the booze and the pot, just the fact that a part of me gets off on Michael's visits I'm sure rates me a room at some facility. But did the actual dissolution of my good sense happen when I met Michael, or when he came back? I used to think being Michael's girlfriend was fate, instead of the dumb luck it really was. And if I'd taken that job busing tables at the country club instead of babysitting the twins that summer, it's doubtful I ever would've registered on Michael's radar.

How was I to know Michael Green was moving next door to Sam and Ethan? I may be crazy, but I'm not psychic. And I've wished a million times I'd let Sam and Ethan stay inside watching cartoons the day he moved in, but I just *had* to see what the new neighbors' stuff was like.

All I can remember now is that when the moving van pulled away, Michael came out and stood there on his front steps, and I swear he was brighter than the summer sky. He looked around his yard, taking everything in, and then he turned to us and waved. I all but froze solid in the heat when I realized he was coming over. He hopped over the hedgerow and walked across the lawn, and the boys ran over to Michael—a complete stranger—and started talking to him like he was their big brother home from college!

In minutes they had told Michael all about their parents' work schedule, the prissy eight-year-old girl across the street they were secretly in love with, and that they had six cans of fruit cocktail stashed under their porch in case of an emergency.

It had taken me two weeks to get more than one-word answers out of them.

But that's just the way it was with Michael. He was a person who sucked you into his life the moment you met him, and you felt like you'd known him forever.

And solemn Ethan—it was like he'd found a puppy to play with and couldn't wait to show it off. He grinned this huge lopsided grin and dragged Michael to the porch steps while Sam crashed through the gardens looking for a ball, yelling, "Wait! Don't go anywhere, I know there's one here."

I should have yelled at Sam to stop trampling the flowers. But I didn't. I wanted him to find a ball. I didn't want Michael to go, either.

"I'm Michael. Michael Green," he said, smiling at me like I was something worth smiling about. "And these two can't be related to you, not with those incredible blue eyes."

I was amazed that in those few seconds he'd noticed my eyes were different from the twins. My cheeks blazed, and I hoped it didn't show through my already sunburned skin. I remember the overpowering smell of coconut lotion drifting around him, and how I wished I had taken more time getting dressed that morning—how I wished I were wearing coconut lotion, too.

"I'm Jordan, and these hyperactive nine-year-olds are way too coordinated to be related to me. I'm just watching Sam and Ethan for the summer."

I couldn't believe how calm I sounded when my heart was racing. How could I talk so easily to this gorgeous creature I didn't even know? I asked myself this question later, but I knew the answer. It was all Michael. He was magic.

"Yeah." Ethan laughed. "We were hoping we'd get some boy to watch us."

Sam jogged up the steps next to Michael. "Yeah, she sucks at throwing a ball!" He tossed the muddy football he'd found over his head and Michael leaned over and snatched it with one large hand.

"Go long!" Michael barked. He barely moved his arm, but the ball sailed in a straight line all the way over the hedges and crashed into the far side of Michael's yard. "That'll keep them busy for a few minutes," he said, laughing as the twins ran screaming after it.

"So," he said, getting up, "I'll teach you how to throw a pass if you'll show me the hot spots around here." He winked as he picked my book up off the porch swing and sat down next to me. He flipped through the pages, and then tossed it carelessly onto the wood floor. "Do you go to North Shore?"

The swing was small, and my skin burned where his leg pressed against mine. The coconut smell filled my head.

"Um, yeah. I'll be a junior." Any sense of calm I'd felt was totally gone. I mean, his leg was right there wedged up against mine, and the pressure was revving my heart and scrambling my brain.

"Cool. I've got a car, but I'm in need of a tour guide. Wanna go for a drive later? You could show me around town, or we could just hang out with your friends."

He pushed his feet against the porch, gently moving the swing into motion. I was grateful for the small breeze cooling my face as I weighed his invitation.

How could I have Michael meet my friends? Rachael, with her short black skirts and black stockings, even in the ninety-degree heat. She'd fawn over him and tell him all about whomever she was sleeping with—what they were doing in bed, or the backseat, or wherever. I could picture her running her fingers through his thick brown hair.

And Janine and Gabby? Did I really want to subject Michael to one of their drunken sing-alongs to *Rent*? He didn't seem like the kind of guy who would appreciate a slurred performance of "Seasons of Love"—or any Broadway song, for that matter.

"My friends work nights. Well, Rachael doesn't, but she's, you know . . . caught up in a new romance. But I could show you around. I get off at five-thirty."

It wasn't a total lie, really. I hadn't seen a lot of Rachael lately—not since she'd hooked up with that loser. I mean, what kind of normal twenty-year-old wants to hang with someone who's sixteen? And Janine and Gabby were busy working at the country club. I just didn't mention that we usually met after hours on the club's fourteenth hole to drink whatever Gabby swiped from the bar.

"Okay, great." He smiled and rubbed his hand down my thigh. "Just you and me." He jumped up suddenly and caught the football before it slammed into the house.

The twins thundered up the steps, jumping all over Michael and trying to snatch the ball out of his hands.

And that was it. I fell in love with him that day—it was so easy. Everything about Michael was easy. He had this electricity around him. God, he dazzled me—blinded me. I didn't see what was coming. How could I not see what was coming? It should have been obvious from the start that Michael was too big for someone like me.

But I didn't see it, and I spent two months with him; two glorious months that I'm paying for now.

CHAPTER THREE

I guess the key to regaining my sanity lies in excising Michael from my life again. I know now—well, deep down I've always known—that these visits of his are not akin to winning the lottery. They're a nightmare, and they're messing with my head. They're making me contemplate things I could very easily have kept in the dark shadows of my mind without ever bringing them to light.

And I can't trust myself not to open the window some more.

So I'm going to make a list. Lisa would be proud. Well, maybe she'd be proud if the list had more to do with the top ten ways to improve my looks, and less about deep-sixing Michael.

Offing your dead ex-boyfriend? Isn't that redundant, Jordan? Not to mention messy! And you have more important things to worry about, you know. No offense, but have you spent any time in front of a mirror lately? I know you don't want to hear it, but your mom and I still think you're a bit too casual about your appearance, and a list of the top ten cosmetics you should be using would be way more appropriate than tangling with a former prom king! Do you still have that list I made you in seventh grade?

I push Lisa's voice out of my head and open the vampire encyclopedia I got out of the library. This is my list. Mine alone.

I get a pencil and paper and open the book to the page I'd marked: "How to Dispose of a Vampire."

Top ten ways to get rid of Michael Green:
1. Submerge in water (bathtub?)
2. Remove the heart (avoid blood splatter)

Yeah, right.

A gust whips under the windowsill, rustling the paper sitting on my bedside table. I shake my head. Making that list was a joke. There's no way I can pull off any of that stuff, and my heart is beating double time anticipating the jolt I get when Michael pops up at the window. I crumple the paper up and toss it in the trash.

I reach under my bed for the peach schnapps I snagged from the liquor cabinet. I hate drinking stuff this sweet, but one of my mother's stupid Mahjong buddies always brings a bottle, so it's not as likely to be missed, compared to one of the eighty-freaking-dollar bottles of wine my stepfather collects. I make a mental note to add it to my list of booze for Adam to replace when he gets home for winter break. I take a couple of swigs, grimacing as it burns its way down my throat.

Lights out. I flop back onto my pillow and pull the comforter up to my chin. It's getting colder every night, and the schnapps is warming only my belly. I reach my hand out to shut the window, but pull it back, wondering which part of me is stronger, the part that's tempted to let Michael in, or the part that wishes he'd just disappear? That's what I really want him to do. If he disappears, I can get on with my sorry little existence and not have to think so much.

I mean, picturing myself drowning Michael in a bathtub or heading out into the night and coming home with his heart in my backpack is laughable. And there are some very compelling reasons to let him in. Just the thought of not having to deal with school or my mother's crap makes the prospect appealing—never mind the fact my life sucks, and that in itself would be enough to seal the deal.

So why haven't I let him in?

Rachael shouldn't have asked *"Have you always been a head case?"* The real question is, when did things get so bad that letting Michael in is something I might contemplate?

"Jordan, let me in."

I draw a quick breath and my heart takes it up

another notch. "God, Michael, can't you at least cough? You scare the hell out of me every time you do that. You need a bell."

"Let me in, I'm so cold. I miss you. I can't stand being so close and not being able to hold you. You used to fit so perfectly in my arms."

My stomach flutters like it did the first time he kissed me. I start to smile, but realize getting gushy over every little thing coming out of his mouth is counterproductive to clear thinking. I may be waffling about the whole opening-the-window thing, but it's not in my best interest to get swept away by compliments. I need to be tough.

"Look, Michael, I know this is usually where I do my 'Go away, I'll never let you in' bit, but I'm worried our relationship is getting stale. You know, same old conversation every night? We're like some B-listers in a horror movie being overplayed on the Sci-Fi Channel. I really think we need to shake things up a bit, recapture some of the spontaneity we once had." .

"Real nice! You're not the one stuck out here every night. You're not the one whose life was destroyed."

"You're totally right, Michael. I'm an insensitive ass and I don't know why you put up with me. Perhaps you'd have better luck skulking outside Neela Nelson's window. She's the one you started dating after me— the very day we broke up, I believe. If you're doing this stalking thing in chronological order, it only makes sense to try her next. Who knows, maybe she lives in a ranch and you won't have to mess with a tree."

Michael sighs, and I look out the window. I can tell he's running his hands through his hair. I try not to think about how I used to play with his curls, or the way my bare skin burned under his hands.

"You know Neela doesn't matter. She never did. It's you I came back for. Doesn't that mean anything?"

"Yeah, well, pardon me if I'm feeling more trapped than flattered. I had to blow off working on the fall play, I couldn't join the cross-country team, and I never see my friends anymore because I need to be home before dark! Sorry, Michael, I'm just not feeling the love."

"You don't need to hide from me. I'd never hurt you. I'd never force you to do anything you didn't want to do."

A laugh escapes from my mouth. Never force me to do anything I didn't want to do, huh? I guess technically he hadn't, but all the same, having your new boyfriend's very large hands shoved down your pants on the first date falls on the forceful side of things, I think. But I didn't say no, I didn't say anything. I just let it happen.

"Look, Jordan, let's talk about something else. How's school? Are you still hanging out with the Diva Twins?"

"They hated when you called them that. Do you even remember their names?"

"Uh, Abby and Janine?"

"*Gabby* and Janine. And you only remember Janine because you were friends with her brother."

"Yeah, *Gabby*, whatever. But you can't tell me they

aren't divas. You all but laughed your ass off the first time I called them that, because you know it's true."

"Well, every group's got to have its hierarchy. Yours had Marnie Shaw and you, of course. And, as Gabby and Janine have the best voices, they get to be the drama club queens—literally. At least they don't lord it over the whole school."

Michael snorts. "Like they could. Like you're even into hanging out with them. All you used to do was bitch about them."

"We were in the middle of the summer show and they were being, well, divas." He laughs and a smile warms my face. "And if you'd gone to see the show with me you'd know that *Bye Bye Birdie* doesn't really have a standout female lead, and . . ."

"And even though there wasn't a real star, they each fought like hell to become one. Yeah, yeah, I remember."

"I sometimes wondered if you were paying attention, I mean, musicals not being on your top ten list of ways to spend an evening, unless it was 'the top ten things worse than being—'"

"Dead."

"You hate musicals that much?"

"I'd rather eat glass."

He's laughing, but I feel like I've been insulted. I try to remember what common ground we had.

"Or kiss Marjory Stiles."

"Gross, Michael! Stop! Enough, I get it. But to clarify things, the Divas and I do share a lot of interests. We're all in the drama club and we all have parents who could care less what we do or where we are, and they know the people to buy pot from. And Rachael? Well, Rachael and I have a lot in common." Even I have to roll my eyes at that one.

"You're so full of shit! You and Miss I'm-in-Desperate-Need-of-an-Extreme-Makeover are worlds apart. I sure as hell could never see why you were hanging around with that Mohawked freak."

Why do I hang out with any of them? I've wondered that myself. Yeah, we like shows, but Gabby has a mean streak, and Janine, well, she's a little dim and it kind of bugs me that she's never finished a book. Rachael drives me crazy with her endless quest for self-improvement, but bottom line is they're willing to hang out with me and that's better than being alone. And there's that whole thing about our parents not giving a damn what we do. It's very convenient to hang out until all hours when nobody has a curfew and there's no one to do a breath check when you do stumble home.

Not that I will admit this to Michael. He doesn't need to know that I haven't had a real friend since Lisa.

"I'll have you know that Rachael grew her Mohawk out over the summer. But let's talk about you. How deep were your relationships? I could tell you were real tight with Steve and Eric. I mean, the way you guys constantly slugged each other in the arm was obviously a sign of great affection. Not to mention your very public grope sessions with various cheerleaders, model wannabes, and jockettes. They weren't the epitome of deep, if you know what I mean."

"Look, I never said I had anything great going on. Never. Why do you think I'm here with you? I don't go to Neela's or Ashley's or Monica's. I'm here, here with you. You were the only one that got me, and I'll wait as long as it takes until you admit we belong together."

I want to believe him, I really, really do. But he moved on so fast. How could he if I really was *the one*?

Of course I was ready to move on with Danny last summer, and if Michael hadn't come back, I would have. But at least I waited ten months before I started hooking up again. Well, hooking up seriously. I don't want to dwell on the other hooking up I've done. And it doesn't really count since I'm always pretty trashed when it happens. But what I've done is nothing compared to the sheer number of girls Michael was with. I had to watch him laugh and flirt with girl after girl—he didn't even look at me in the halls. How much could I have meant?

"Be honest, Jo, what do you have going on that's worth hanging around this lame town for?"

I keep my mouth shut because there's no way I'm going to tell Michael he's not the only guy that gets my pulse racing, that I get to my Comparative Lit class early so I can watch Danny Douglas walk in, that I hope I'll get another chance with Danny and maybe that's why I'm hanging on?

"You can't tell me you'd really miss your family. I know you can't stand your mother, and your dad's, what, three states away? Heard from him lately? Then there's your brother—quite the stellar guy. Who wouldn't miss a big brother who'd buy booze for his underage sister and then let her get so trashed she pukes in her room? Are you feeling *that* love? And let's see . . . Rachael, Janine, and *Gabby*? They don't even know you, Jordan. They don't even care. I'm the only one who cares."

His words slice into my stomach. It's bad enough getting crap about my life from Rachael, but at least she's trying to help. Michael's just trying to cram salt in an open wound; make it bigger, make it fester. But I'm not there yet. I'm not ready to give up. "Go away, Michael."

"You know it's true. I'm all you have. Just ask me in."

"Get the hell out of my tree."

I want to shut the window, but I'm scared to get too close to him. I've dreamed about him reaching through the opening too many times. I've dreamed that when he touches me, I turn to ice.

"Get a clue, Jordan. Nobody cares. I'm the only one."

"What about you, Michael? Do you miss your friends? Your family? How do you feel now that you can never go back? How does it feel knowing everyone is moving on just fine?"

"Fuck you!"

He breaks a branch and throws it at my window. I draw back and watch him jump away.

I count to ten, then reach out and close the window.

"Right back at you."

CHAPTER FOUR

I see Rachael standing at the corner waiting for me. She waves, and I swallow hard. Her hair is bright purple. I guess she's forgoing the extreme haircuts in favor of extreme color. Her hair is almost down to her shoulders, and the way the wind is whipping it around, it looks like she's got a sea anemone sprouting from her head. Purple is not a good color on Rachael. I consider being mean and telling her about the "under the sea" vibe she's sending, but then she smiles, and I remember to feel grateful I've got someone to walk to school with.

"New color, huh?" There, that was perfect—a noncommittal acknowledgement of the bizarre new hue that leaves her feelings intact.

"Yeah, but what's up with you? You look like hell,"

Rachael says as I get close. "Don't you sleep anymore?"

Touché.

I reconsider the sea anemone analogy, but bite my tongue and start walking. "I haven't been feeling well, I guess." Our boots click in unison, and the sound calms me. I contemplate telling her that Michael's been visiting me the last three months, and even though I haven't let him in, he's sucking me dry all the same, but I know it's one thing to look like crap and another to sound crazy.

"Well, maybe you should lay off the smokes for a while. Detox your system. You know, like I did that seaweed-and-water-purification regime. It got me back on track, and I can party harder than before."

"I think I'll manage okay," I mumble. "You know me, not much of a seaweed kind of gal."

Rachael drives me crazy sometimes. If she's not doing her self-help guru spiel, she's pushing some diet or colon cleanser on us. How can someone be a radical vegetarian and not eat two-thirds of the food chain, but still throw back shots, snort lines, and get stoned—that's healthy?

"I think I know what your problem is." She stops walking and turns to me. Her eyes are wide, and I can tell she thinks she's on to some life-altering stuff. "We talked about it in Bell's class on Friday."

Oh, no. I should have known it would just get worse when she signed up for Psych II. I wonder if the administration is aware of how much Mr. Bell deviates from the text so he can play shrink for all the hot girls in class. What I don't get is why Rachael's buying into it. I know she has a thing for all this nonsense, but Mr. Bell taught European history for fifteen years before he switched to psych, and it's so obvious he's making half the stuff up as he goes along.

"Please, Rachael, not another Bell diagnosis." I start down the sidewalk, hoping to stop this before Rachael morphs into her version of Dr. Phil. "Isn't it enough I've sat through several lengthy discussions about my ongoing battle with social anxiety disorder—like it's so out there to have a major problem talking to the jerks that populate our school? But do tell, what's next? Purple-hair envy?"

Rachael's boots grind to a halt. I half expect to see clouds of smoke puff up from the sidewalk.

"Oh, that's real nice. For your information, Jordan, I've been getting a lot of books from the bookstore, so it's not just parroting back some high school class jargon. Like you'd ever dare mess with the sweet, wholesome façade you're sporting. And at least I'm honest; at least people aren't scratching their heads wondering who the hell the real me is!"

Rachael doubles her pace and I have to hustle to catch up with her. So much for the soothing rhythm of boot clicks.

I've seen Rachael's book collection and find it hard to believe that *Reviving Ophelia* or *Queen Bees and Wannabes* would have useful advice pertaining to my real problem: Michael. But I don't want to piss her off any more than I already have. "Rachael, I'm sorry. I'm not sleeping well and I guess I've really been on edge, and I shouldn't take it out on you." I run ahead and stand directly in her path. "Please—you've got to help! What's my problem?"

Rachael stops and scowls. "Like you're really interested?"

"I am."

"Fine. You're depressed. Though I'm not sure if you have major depression or this dys-something disorder. Either way, you need help. And for your information, lack of sleep is a *major* symptom."

"Like this is news? Like I haven't chronicled my downward spiral into teen hell in my journals?"

"I'm serious, Jordan. You've got the symptoms."

"I'm serious, too. I filled out the depression checklist in Mr. Callahan's health class last month, and you know what? From the looks on the faces of ninety percent of the class, I'd say I'm part of a very big club."

Rachael starts walking again, shaking her head. I should've just nodded and asked what I could do to help myself. Whenever I piss her off, she comes up with some excuse to ditch me the minute we get in the school doors, and I have to go to my locker alone. I've admitted to myself that I do have some sort of social anxiety problem, but she knows I know it, and I think it is the height of cruelty to desert someone with my condition.

"Rachael, wait!" I match her quick strides and wish my legs were as long as hers. My breath comes out in short wheezes and I curse myself for blowing off the cross-country team this season, and for smoking so much pot. "Slow down, okay?"

She turns sharply and puts her hands on her hips. "You know, Jordan, I'm just trying to help. You never go out anymore. You never call. You're like a completely different person. I really needed you last month when Thomas and I broke up, but you couldn't be bothered to call. Nobody called."

Oh, silly me! This isn't about Rachael being concerned because it's obvious I'm about to self-implode. This is about Rachael being bummed out because I wasn't around to pick up her shattered ego and bring her back into the group.

Gabby and Janine never tolerate her I'm-done-with-my-current-boyfriend-so-now-I-can-hang-out-with-you-guys-on-the-weekend-again routine. They like her to suffer awhile, and it's always been my job to convince them that Rachael's learned her lesson and deserves to be let back in the fold. They'd come around eventually, but apparently I've shirked my negotiator duties, and reassimilation into the group is taking longer than Rachael is used to.

Is she even aware that I've been missing in action on the weekends for three months, that I only see Janine and Gabby at school? What does she want from me?

She's still staring, waiting for the expected groveling. Part of me wants to tell Rachael to go screw herself because I've got enough trouble negotiating the opening of my stupid window with my stupid ex-boyfriend—I wonder what Mr. Bell would have to say about that—and part of me is terrified I'll blow this standoff and end up walking to school alone for the rest of the year. Gosh, I wonder why I'm depressed!

"Things have been extra screwy at home," I say finally. I look down at the sidewalk, kick some acorns into the grass for effect, and take a deep breath. "And Steve has been a major pain. He's been fighting with my mom twenty-four seven for blowing all his money on things she doesn't need, and I guess I'm just not handling it well."

All of this is true, but really, it's strictly status quo—nothing to keep me up at night. I'm just hoping a little sympathy will help patch things up. She's still staring and arching her oh-so-pointy plucked eyebrows, so I know I've got to come up with more, and with only one block separating me from the source of my social anxiety disorder, I've got to think fast.

"And I don't know," I add, doing the big, sad, puppy-eye thing. "I just haven't been able to shake this mood I've been in. I feel like I'm stuck, and nothing helps."

Having taken Psych I last spring with Rachael, I know that I've gotten past the admitting-I-have-a-problem stage. I just need to play into her need to rescue others, and make helping poor little me as painless as possible.

"And I guess I have been spending too much time by myself. But maybe you could come over this weekend and we could do something. Maybe a makeover and some of my mom's dresses will get me out of this funk. We haven't done that in ages." I give her a hopeful look. Her eyes light up, and I smile.

Gotcha!

"Only if you let me wear the green snake-print dress! It's so bizarre, it's cool. Where does your mom wear those things to anyway?" she asks, starting toward school. "And why does she need so many of them? I mean, really, twenty-odd dresses with a variety of feathers, fringe, and sequins? Your mom is so channeling some Vegas showgirl or something."

We head across the school parking lot with a more relaxed *click-clack* pace. Disaster averted. And really, as much as I'd never be caught out of the house in my mom's makeup and clothes, it is fun to dress up. I just need to make sure Rachael is out by—I take a quick peek inside my planner where I've taped the sunset tables—6:29. I'll need to get Rachael to leave a bit before then, because I have no idea when my dearly departed boyfriend starts hanging around the house.

I wonder if Michael would like the black dress with the slit that goes up almost to the top of my thigh. It would be fun to surprise him. Or maybe the blue flapper dress with the fringe might set a lighter tone for our nightly chat.

"Where's your mom going to be?" Rachael asks.

I feel my cheeks burn. "Oh, uh, just some christening upstate; one of Steve's relatives. They're spending the weekend."

I'm glad Rachael can't read my mind. What is wrong with me, anyway? It is completely twisted to even contemplate dressing up for Michael. And, as of last night, I'm not even on speaking terms with him.

Paging Dr. Bell.

"Hey, check it out." Rachael pulls my arm back and points toward the school. "Look who's back from a lengthy stay at rehab, and look at the chill passing over the fountain crowd!"

I follow Rachael's finger and see Lisa getting out of her father's antique Porsche. I'd started to wonder if Lisa was ever coming back, but there she is, gently shutting the door and nervously scanning the front courtyard. It's weird to see her so tentative, weird to see her taking baby steps across the lot, because Lisa always had this springy bounce to her step.

Her tennis buds and cheerleader friends are perched on their usual spots along the fountain's edge, but they're all huddled and whispery. The moment Lisa steps up onto the sidewalk, all but two of them quickly swing their backpacks over their shoulders and scurry en masse up the front steps.

"Oh my God, what are they doing?" I'm totally taken aback. Lisa was a central figure in that group; I can't believe a stay in rehab would make them shut her out.

"Didn't you hear?" Rachael hisses, leaning in closer to me. "Lisa is a total pariah now. All the *über*jocks' parents have forbidden their star athletes to come in contact with Lisa lest they pick up her nasty coke habit."

I shake my head. "What do they think, Lisa was snorting all by herself?"

"Doesn't matter, Lisa was the only one that went to rehab, so they can imagine their kids are clean."

"Maybe Courtney will come through," I say, tilting my head toward the fountain.

Lisa walks over to her doubles partner, Courtney, and Courtney's best friend, Alicia. They appear to be so engrossed in their conversation that they don't notice Lisa standing right in front of them. My God, they're sitting in Lisa's shadow, why can't they at least acknowledge her presence? My stomach pinches itself into a tight knot. I want to rescue her, but finally Courtney looks up and gets this wide-eyed, surprised look, like she can't believe it's Lisa and not a solar eclipse that's cast her in shadow. She plasters a big smile on her face and jumps up, giving Lisa the "Oh my God, when did you get back?" routine.

I guess she doesn't want to blow her chance to be Lisa's partner again, because she sure won't make it to the state all-star team without her. Alicia barely manages a tight smile, and they walk awkwardly into the school.

Rachael and I follow at a safe distance. Dr. Deluca greets us as we go in and gives us his daily, "Ladies," with a nod and quick check of our eyes. Doesn't he know the people who have taken the time to get stoned before school flush their eyes with Visine and use the side entrance by the gym?

The door swings shut behind us. Rachael mumbles something about her Latin teacher and hooks a sharp left toward the language wing. I want to believe she has actual business with her Latin teacher, but I know this is her way of punishing me for the "purple-hair envy" comment.

My stomach turns again and I head to my locker alone, bracing myself for hallway anxiety. I know walking to one's locker is a relatively simple thing to do. It is, after all, an extremely common activity that everyone does many times a day, everyday. And by the end of the day it doesn't even bother me that much, but there's something about that first walk through the halls, knowing people are rating my hair, my clothes, my every move. The buzz is deafening as everyone is giving a fresh check on everyone else. It makes my throat close up. When I'm with Rachael, I'm okay; I can pretend to be like her and not care what anyone thinks. Alone, I freak.

Do I:

A. Focus my eyes on the floor and plow through the halls like I've got something so urgent to do that nothing else matters?

B. Take furtive glances ahead and make quick eye contact with random members of the student body, despite the looks I may get in return, because after Sissy Burns stuck her tongue out at me freshman year, I've learned some people just don't like being looked at.

C. Put on the Miss America smile and beam at everyone like I'm totally stoked to be here and see everyone?

Or:

D. None of the above; just walk down the hallway like a normal person, because deep down I know that no one cares that I'm simply walking to my locker?

I decide option A will produce the least amount

of adrenaline and start watching shoes go past. I take quick peeks up so I don't run into any other people keeping their eyes to the ground. As I'm rounding the last corner, I hear footsteps coming up quickly behind me. Two arms link with mine and I am enormously relieved to see Gabby and Janine on either side.

There's just no getting past having friends to walk down the hallways with; it shows the world that even though you've been labeled quiet, or shy, or just plain weird, you're capable of having relationships with other people, unlike the Marjory Stiles of the world who wander around alone, reduced to mumbling into their hands during lunch period because it's a better option than talking to the actual lunch being served that day.

"Did Miss Purple Mountains Majesty ditch you?" Gabby asks.

"Yeah." I laugh, hoping to convince them that I am in no way bothered by her desertion. "Do you think you two could call her? She's all on my case."

Gabby whips out her cell phone. "I'll call for an appointment at the salon so they can strip that heinous color from her hair! She was just approaching normal, and then she comes to school looking like a freakin' eighties refugee. I guess the Goth garb wasn't pulling in the stares like it used to, and she had to kick it up a notch."

Janine pats me on the shoulder. "If she's still bent on Monday, I'll drive you to school so you won't be alone in the big bad halls."

"Like I care about that," I say, pretending not to know what she's talking about.

Gabby laughs. "You were walking down the hall like a hunchback. For a minute I thought you were Marjory Stiles."

So much for that air of important business I was hoping to project. "Well, I happen to find high school footwear immensely fascinating."

"Never mind shoes, we've got news," Gabby says, eyes gleaming.

"Lisa?" I say smugly. I love beating her to the punch. It happens so rarely.

"Damn, who told you?"

"I saw her get dropped off this morning."

Gabby is clearly disappointed and drops my arm. "Well, did you know that she's no longer the IT girl?"

"Yep." I nod. "Saw the fountain crowd royally blow her off just a few minutes ago."

"Damn!" she says again. "I would've stayed back and watched your Quasimodo routine if I'd have known you'd scoop my poop!"

Janine squeezes my arm. "I still love you. And since she's an old friend of yours, I was thinking we should ask Lisa to hang out with us, or have lunch or something." Janine drops my other arm as we walk up to our section of peach-colored lockers.

"Nice," I say. "But you can't really ask someone who just got out of rehab to hang out with people who spend the majority of their free time getting wasted. Unless, of course, you're ready to get clean and sober?"

We all laugh and start spinning our locks. Rachael saunters by and leans against her locker, smiling coolly.

"What's so funny?" she asks.

"Your hair," Gabby says.

Rachael's eyes go wide, and some of the kids around us start snickering. Janine snorts and sticks her head into her locker to stifle a laugh.

"I'm just kidding. It looks great. Really."

Rachael turns to me, and from the nasty look I'm getting, it's clear Gabby's not the one she'll take this out on. She stretches her spine to her full five-foot-nine Amazonian height and gives me a long glare. Me!

"You know, Jordan, I just remembered I have plans for Saturday. Sunday, too."

She flips her stupid purple hair, twists her lock back and forth, and opens the door, pulling out her trig book and calculator. She slams the door and stalks down the hall.

"Send Barney my love," Gabby calls after her, cracking up.

Rachael holds her hand behind her back and gives us the finger.

Janine frowns. "Who's Barney?"

"The big purple dinosaur?" Gabby looks hopeful.

"Enough already! Why do you have to torment her?" I ask, trying to figure out how it is that Rachael thinks any of that scene was my fault—unless she's still mad about my earlier dig.

"I'll talk to her at lunch," Gabby says. "I'll bet the stash I picked up will soften the heart of the warrior princess. And by the way, when will you be joining us for fun and such? It's bad enough you ditched the play, the sets totally suck."

I turn to my locker to grab a book.

"Yeah," Janine says, "we haven't seen much of you lately."

"It's just that you guys get out of work so late and I've been babysitting the twins a lot lately."

Gabby narrows her eyes. "Those people go out a lot."

I can tell from her tone that my excuses are ghostly thin after three months.

"Yeah, well, their father's doing a lot of business entertaining." This is a total lie. I haven't watched the twins since Michael's reappearance, but until I figure out what to do about him, I want to make sure Janine and Gabby don't think I'm blowing them off. The last thing I need is to have them redirect their attention to me.

Aha! The lightbulb goes off over my head. Is this why Rachael's so mad, because I've never stuck up for her when Gabby is doing her Queen Bee routine? Honestly, Rachael gets enough crap from a large part of the student body. I guess it hurts when your friends are dishing it out, too. And it must also hurt when you know one of your friends is keeping her mouth shut because she wants to fly under the radar.

Ick! I felt much better when I thought I was the victim of an unprovoked attack.

"Well, Mark Menducci is throwing a bash Saturday, and you're coming!" Janine says. "We even got off work!"

I'm not sure how any of us know Mark, but he has these megaparties and invites the theater group from our school. It's like a teen version of Pleasure Island from *Pinocchio* at his house: heated pool, Jacuzzis, video games, pinball machines, pot, coke, kegs, and—most importantly—no parents. I still don't remember how I got home from the last party. Of course, that was last spring, before Michael came back from the dead and I was still going out and having fun.

I plaster on a smile and force my eyes into an *"Oh my God, can't wait"* look. "Don't worry, I'll be there! I need a night out!"

What I really need is a good excuse, because there is no way I'm venturing out after sunset with Michael lurking around.

"Good!" Janine says. "And I'll walk you to class so you don't have to stare at people's shoes. Like there are any good ones to look at, anyway."

"Later, chicks." Gabby shuts her locker with her hip and heads off in the other direction.

Janine and I round the corner and I see Danny peering into his locker. I wonder if we can sneak by unnoticed.

"Hey, Danny!" Janine hollers. "Look who's here? Jordan!"

Danny looks our way and I can feel the blood rushing to my cheeks. I plaster on another smile. "Hey," I mumble, rushing past him.

I think he mumbles something about seeing me in class, but it's too hard to hear with Janine cackling in my ear.

"What'd you do that for?" I hiss as we pass the next set of lockers.

"The poor guy is pining away for you. I told you he's in the play—finally someone tall enough to dance with Ashley Hannigan—but it's so obvious he tried out hoping to see you."

"I seriously doubt that." I seriously hope it's true!

"Well, it's not too late to help with the sets—they really do suck. I wish you could've done the design."

"Me too, but I'll try to get Saturday night off for the party," I lie.

"Danny's coming," Janine sings.

"Really?"

"Really! So find a way to be there."

Janine chatters on, but my mind is racing. Maybe I could go to the party. Mark Menducci lives in Sands Point, forty minutes from my house. Michael will be expecting me to be home. I'll make sure I'm out of the house long before sunset. Even if he could track me down, he wouldn't risk showing up and being seen by everyone.

Of course, even if I do hook up with Danny, I'll still have to deal with Michael.

God! Why did Michael have to come back?

CHAPTER FIVE

I remember everything about July 6th: the smells, the heat, the sound of the birds in the tree. Every detail is scored into my brain because that was the day Michael came back to haunt me.

The air in my room was sticky and hot, and I was trying not to feel pissed that my mom kept "forgetting" to get me a new air conditioner, despite six trips to the mall that week. I mean, Michael had been dead for two days, what right did I have to bitch about the heat?

I heard the AC in my mom's room humming and thought of heading in there, but decided sweating was better than dealing with her.

As if on cue, she opened my door. "Oh, Jordan, you've been moping for two days. You should take this as a sign to move on. It's not normal for a girl your age to have had only one boyfriend."

"Ah, so you finally admit you don't think I'm normal," I said, hoping for some sort of an apology, or at least some clarification.

My mother just stared, shaking her head. She picked some clothes off the floor and tossed them into my hamper. "I don't suppose you've thought any more about doing something special tomorrow? You could invite some friends over; I could get a cake."

"Mom!"

"I know! I know! God forbid you should have a birthday party. You'd think it was a crime being the center of attention for a few hours! Couldn't you at least invite Lisa over? Surely you two can get past your big blowup after all this time? And I, for one, would love to see someone other than Miss Mohawk at the house."

"Rachael's growing out her Mohawk. It sort of just sticks out everywhere now."

My mother shook her head again. "At least you've shown some sense and haven't followed Rachael's misbegotten footsteps. And I still think you could learn a thing or two from Lisa; she knows what school is for. It's to get involved, to be a part of something. I would have killed to have your opportunities when I was your age."

I had to bite my tongue to stop myself from telling her the rumor about Lisa. It was tempting, though, if only to see the bug-eyed look she reserves for whatever getup Rachael has on, but it was too damn hot to get into something else with her.

All I could do was hope that sometime soon she'd get over the big "Lisa blowup." Not that we even had a blowup, but Mom is a born embellisher, and I guess from her perspective that sounded better than what really happened. Lisa liked cheering and sports, big crowds and hair and makeup, and I loathed all of that. She found new friends; I found new friends—the end. But Mom's convinced Lisa dumped me in some dramatic fashion because I "don't get what high school is all about."

I think the real reason she was so bent about the whole Lisa thing is that, unlike me, Lisa actually likes my mother and thinks that being obsessed with clothes and makeup is part of the natural order of things. Hell, Lisa thought I was lucky to have a mom who knew what was in style.

I always thought Lisa and I were prime candidates for a switched-at-birth investigation.

But I missed Lisa, too, sometimes. The old Lisa, the one who liked to read the same books I did and imagined fairies swimming in her pool. I even missed those stupid lists she was always making. And Lisa's family—a nice, totally normal family—I missed having dinner with them. They actually made a point of eating together most nights of the week.

But I guess things at Lisa's house weren't too keen, because Lisa left for rehab the day after Michael died.

I picked up a book, hoping Mom would get the hint

and leave, but she sat down on my bed and put her hand on my knee. It was all I could do not to cringe. She had that serious look on her face that meant she was about to impart some wonderful words of wisdom that I would find either ridiculous or offensive, or both.

"You know, Michael might have stuck around longer if you spruced yourself up a bit. You're such a pretty girl, you just need a little blush, a little color."

She reached out and ran her long red fingernails through my hair, and I knew she was wishing I would get those highlights she's always talking about.

"And hanging around with someone like Rachael probably didn't help. I still can't believe her mother lets her out of the house looking like the star attraction from some freak show. Of course, it's probably just as well you weren't dating him anymore. God knows he might have pulled one of those murder-suicide stunts. I hope the next boy will be a little more stable." She shook her head. "And he was such a good-looking boy."

"Yeah, usually it's the ugly people that are suicidal." I glared at my mother, wanting her to realize how stupid the things coming out of her mouth were. But she didn't notice. She just got up and started picking up clothes again.

I know I shouldn't hate my mother for having such a warped take on things. It was really hard for her growing up with Grandma Stein, who was a total head case who went through four husbands before Mom was ten years old. But, God, Mom's forty-seven years old now; she should have been in and out of therapy and functioning like a rational adult already.

"Oh, no!" she moaned. "This is imported linen, Jordan," she said, waving a wrinkled white shirt toward me, "and you've destroyed it by wadding it up on the floor like that!"

My mother held the shirt away from her body like it was one of the dead moles the cat is always sneaking in. Not that she'd ever consider picking one of them up. That's my job.

"I don't even know if the dry cleaner can salvage this. Eighty dollars wasted because you couldn't remember what a hanger is for! If you can't respect my things, I'll ask you to stay out of my closet, young lady."

Shut up, shut up, shut up, I silently begged. I wanted her stupid, unnaturally pink frosted mouth to stop moving. I wanted to yell at her, I wanted to scream, *"What is wrong with you? Michael is dead and all you can do is talk about clothes?"* But instead I said, quietly, "Gabby, Rachael, and Janine will be here soon. I need to get ready for the funeral."

"Fine! I was heading out to get some wine anyway. Steve and I are going to the Gambino's for dinner tonight, and he doesn't think they rate one of his good bottles. Do you need money to get something for yourself?"

"No. Janine's mom is cooking us dinner."

Janine's mother may not care a whole lot about what Janine does, but at least she makes sure there's a hot dinner on the table every night—even if Janine ends up eating it alone most of the time.

"I don't know how that woman finds time to cook. Well, just make sure you don't get anything on my dress." She ran her hand down the navy blue dress hanging on my bedpost, smiling at it like buying it was some great feat she had accomplished. "Why don't you take a change of clothes? And try some of that new green concealer under your eyes before you go. It won't look green when you put it on; it just neutralizes the redness around your eyes. You're just like me: You look awful when you've been crying." My mom smiled. "And don't worry, I know some boy is probably waiting in the wings to snatch you up."

She gave me a knowing look, like we'd just shared something deep, and I used every bit of my willpower to keep from rolling my eyes. "The day I am just like you is the day I will do myself in," I whispered after she left. "And I have a new boyfriend, at least I think I do."

I hoped Danny was going to be at the funeral. He'd left four messages on my machine. I just hadn't gotten up the nerve to call him back. I thought it would just be easier to see him in person. Of course I knew hooking up with a guy at my ex's funeral was all kinds of wrong, but I had figured it was my best shot. I think that's the main difference between my mom and me: I know I have issues, but she just thinks everyone else does.

When I heard the front door shut, I peeked out my window and saw Mom get in her car. Once she pulled away, the grackles that spend the summer in the tree started screeching. I could usually tune them out, but they were hopping around croaking more than usual. I searched the ground until I spotted my cat lounging under the tree, ignoring the ruckus above.

"Nutty, go somewhere else!" I yelled through the screen. He looked up and blinked, then rolled over and went back to sleep. The birds were going nuts, so I shut the window. There wasn't a breeze, anyway.

I got up and walked over to my bookshelf. I picked up a picture of Lisa and me at Sea Cliff Beach. We were twelve, smiling and trying desperately to look sexy despite the fact that our matching bikini tops were completely empty. Exuding sexiness was on a list of "how to get boys to notice us" that Lisa had made. Swimming the length of the beach to impress the lifeguards and making the JV cheerleading squad were also on the list.

Lisa swam every day, and after a few weeks the lifeguards not only noticed her, they took turns racing her. I always watched from the beach because I hated the way my hair dried into sticky strings if I got my head wet in the salt water.

Lisa also made the squad, and I would watch her practice from the stands because I was too scared to try out. That was the summer things started to change.

I pushed *The Phantom Tollbooth* and *National Audubon Society Field Guide to North American Insects and Spiders* apart, and wedged the gold frame in between.

When Gabby, Rachael, and Janine walked into my room later, they all groaned.

"Oh my God! Didn't your mother get you a new air conditioner yet?" Gabby said. "It's like a hundred degrees in here!"

Rachael kicked off her sandals and stretched out on my bed. "Maybe she's subconsciously punishing you for leading a boring life and denying her the chance to live vicariously through you. Or she's just holding out for your birthday."

Janine nodded. "That'd be just like her!"

"I'll take it any way I can get it, and a new unit is better than the clothes she's probably bought me."

Gabby laughed and opened my closet, pulling out a hot pink sweater. "Let's see, is this one from Christmas? You haven't even taken off the tags. And then there's this horror show." She held up a turquoise shirt with sequined flowers.

Rachael grabbed the shirt and held it up to her chest. "Can't you just hear what went through your mom's head when she saw this? 'This shirt is just what Jordan needs to get noticed; maybe it would even inspire her to try out for the cheerleading squad or run for class president!'"

"Hey, I have that shirt," Janine said.

Gabby smirked. "I know."

"Like I said, an air conditioner would be great."

Rachael picked up the book off my bedside table and waved it in front of her face. "Man, don't you have a fan or something? It's almost too hot to smoke in here."

Gabby took a bag of joints out of her purse. "It's *never* that hot."

Rachael flicked a lighter and Gabby took a deep drag. She exhaled and passed the joint to me.

I sucked in and caught a spark before it hit the rug. "I hate doing this in here," I said, forcing the smoke to stay in my lungs. I let out a big breath. "I've imagined my mother coming home and catching us and launching into the drug speech she used to give Adam."

"Get real! Your mom can't say a thing to you." Gabby laughed. "Your brother's been getting openly wasted in the house for years and she hasn't tried to stop him. Unless "the speech" was supposed to guilt him into quitting."

"Yeah, well, he's not here this summer, and if she finds out I smoke I'll have to listen to her where-did-I-go-wrong routine for the next hundred years."

Rachael threw her hands up in the air and shook her head. "'We didn't have all these drugs when I grew up,'" she said in a high, prissy voice. "'What do I know about marijuana? If only you were on antidepressants! That I know!'"

Gabby nodded. "God forbid she'd have to do some actual parenting!"

"God forbid she gets rid of the pharmaceuticals in her bathroom," I said.

Janine sat up and wiggled her eyebrows.

"Don't get any ideas! We just raided them."

"Hello? It's been over a month." Janine pouted.

I shook my head. "Too soon."

"She doesn't keep track of them," Rachael said.

"Well, they're getting low, we'll have to wait until she gets some refills."

Gabby rolled her eyes and handed me the joint. "You're such a wuss!"

I took a deep drag and felt that stupid, stoned smile creep onto my face. "I don't even know why I'm doing this, I hate this feeling, like someone shot my brain full of novocaine."

Gabby laughed. "No one's putting a gun to your head, Jordan."

"Uh, that's a poor choice of words when we're about to go to a funeral," Rachael said.

My stomach gave a nasty turn and my heart beat faster. I was getting totally faced just before Michael's funeral. I'd have to talk to his parents, tell them I was sorry about Michael. Oh God. His mother! Her nasty little dark eyes glaring at me. I didn't think I could face her. Mrs. Green always narrowed her eyes into the smallest of slits that cut right into me, like she knew what we were doing up in my room, and she was sure it'd been all my idea. I imagined the look of disgust on her face as she realized one of the girls who screwed around with her only child—her dead child—had shown up at his funeral wasted.

Part of me wished I had the courage to tell her how much I loved him. That he was my first love. That being with Michael made me feel like I mattered for the first time.

Of course, there's the other part of me that wished I could tell her that I was perfectly happy getting action above the waist until Michael had grabbed my wrist and put my hand down his unzipped pants—and then her darling boy had put his large hands down mine. And, hell, part of me wished I could tell her that once you get your hands down there, you can never go back.

"So," Janine said, finally breaking the silence. "I bet the church is going to be packed. And did you hear they're going to have, like, six counselors at school to help with the 'grieving process.'"

Gabby snorted and choked as smoke sputtered out of her mouth and nose. "I'll bet half the kids at school are thanking God Michael won't be back this fall to lead the Asshole Patrol around."

"Uh, the Asshole Patrol?" I asked. "What's that supposed to mean?"

"Oh, I forgot," Gabby said, placing one hand over her heart. "You loooooved Michael. Well, get a clue, Jordie-pie, Michael was an asshole and you just couldn't see it because you spent a couple of months in a horizontal position with him up in your bedroom. Unless, that is, you preferred to be on top?"

"I always prefer to be on top!" Rachael interjected.

"Cut the crap, you two," Janine said. "And my brother happens to be a member of the so-called 'Asshole Patrol' you're talking about! The guy's dead, so let's, like, drop it."

"Whatever." Gabby jumped off my bed and headed to my bathroom. "But the guy was a major asshole, and you know it!" She shut the door and then opened it again, glaring at us with wide eyes. "And your brother is, too!"

She slammed the door, and I shook my head. "Why is she even going?"

"Are you serious?" Rachael asked, lowering her voice. "She just wants to rip on everyone who'll be there. It's what she lives for. I read about it in this book. People like Gabby get off on putting everyone else down."

That made sense, I thought. Gabby's greatest pleasure was her running social commentary on the haves and have-nots. She spends lunch period analyzing kids—what they're eating, how they're eating it. She's even invented a food pyramid to go along with the school's social hierarchy, like only the bottom feeders openly eat things like egg salad or bologna. And she has a list of superthin girls who eat huge lunches before they head to the bathroom. She waits for them to get up from the table so she can start making puking noises.

Gabby makes me kind of nervous. I always try to leave the cafeteria after she does so she can't say anything about me. But I thought Rachael was right, a funeral would provide scads of sobbing cheerleaders and stoic jocks for Gabby to build a new routine around. Not to mention the nobodies who'll show up, hoping to pass themselves off as close friends of Michael's.

That got me wondering what Michael's friends were going to say about me. Michael and I were only together for a few months, and it's not like Michael did more than grunt in my direction this past year. What would they say about me when they rehashed the funeral tomorrow?

Okay, I told myself. *I have as much right to be at that funeral as the dozens of other girls Michael plowed through in his short time at North Shore High School.*

But I could still hear Marnie Shaw's nasal voice explain her theory of Michael and me in the bathroom one day. It was one of those rotten cosmic timing things. I walked into the girls' room at the end of the science wing during classes, when you can usually pee without the hair nuts hogging the sinks or the Stagano twins harassing someone. Marnie was in one stall and her friend Neela in the other. I could hear a ballpoint pen scraping against the wall, and cigarette smoke was drifting up toward the vent.

"God, I'm so psyched Michael dumped her. I've been trying to get in his pants all summer."

Marnie laughed. "You didn't think it was going to last, did you? She was just the first warm body he met. It's not like she's a skank or anything. She's just a nothing; Michael didn't know any better."

I knew I was the "nothing" Marnie was referring to. And, knowing Neela, she was going to go after Michael with leechlike ferocity. When the toilet flushed, I flew out and back to class. So much for the A-wing bathroom at sixth period.

At least I was Michael's first "nothing."

I turned to Rachael and Janine. "I am too stoned to go to this thing. I can't face Michael's parents and all the teachers who will be there. I can just picture Mr. D stationed at the door looking into everyone's eyes like he does at school."

Janine leered at me. "I think what you mean is you're not stoned enough! And Mr. D will just think your eyes are red because you've been crying."

She handed me the stub of the joint, and like an idiot I took another drag, burning my fingertips.

Cursing, I snuffed the roach out and stared at Janine, wondering how she could get so wasted and still be able to drive her car. I tried driving stoned once—well, I was pretty drunk, too—and I'm still amazed the only thing I hit was the neighbor's hedge. I've always wondered if Mrs. Marx saw the leaves and branches sticking out of the front bumper before I picked them out the following afternoon. Good thing my mom and Steve aren't morning people.

But Janine seems to have no problem driving under the influence. She's our designated drunk driver— literally. I know getting into a car with her is extremely stupid, but she's so confident, and she's never even nicked so much as a small shrub, much less a hedge.

"We need to get some plastic bags to sit on," Janine said. "I left the top down last night and the seats got soaked in that storm."

She stood up and turned around, shaking her wet rear in our faces. Rachael and I burst out laughing, like you can only do when you're stoned.

"You guys liked Michael, didn't you?" I asked when we were quiet again.

"He was hot," Rachael said, shrugging. She got up and grabbed some hair gel off my dresser and ran it through her spiky hair. "I wouldn't have kicked him out of bed!"

Janine shrugged. "He never said much to me, but I guess he was okay."

Gabby opened the bathroom door and cleared her throat. "I had an epiphany while I was sitting on the crapper."

Janine raised an eyebrow. "In English, please?"

"That was English. Anyway, while I was sitting there contemplating the mold on the tiles, I decided it would be a colossal waste of time to go to the funeral of a guy we thought was a waste of oxygen. Well, all of us that didn't have a chance to sample the dearly departed's goods, that is. I say we blow off this farce, purloin a bottle of your mom's cheap vino, and head to Rachael's, where there's central air."

Janine rolled her eyes. "'Purloin'? 'Farce'? I know that's not English!"

"You're right, they're French origin," Rachael said. "And I'm up for skipping it, too. But, I think this is Jordan's call."

Gabby held her hands out, tipping them up and down like a scale. "Boring funeral with teachers present . . . wine and movies?"

I loved Michael, but at that moment the thought of skipping out on his funeral filled me with relief, and since it was Gabby's suggestion, I didn't have to feel so guilty about it. "Wine and movies!"

• • •

Janine nudged me later that evening, and I half opened my eyes. "Home?" I asked, wishing we could just drive around some more and keep listening to the song blasting through the speakers.

"Yeah, you're in luck; looks like your mom and Steve are still out." Janine turned down the volume. "Do you need help getting in?" she asked. "Do you have your key?"

I nodded. "I can do it." The air conditioning was blowing hard and I knew it would be awful getting out into the humid night air. My shorts were cold and damp against my skin: I wished I'd remembered to get a bag to sit on. I wished Janine could remember to put the car roof up at night. I reached out and pulled up the handle and leaned into the door. I stumbled out and bumped the door shut with my hip. I swayed a bit in my driveway and watched Janine drive off.

I fumbled through my purse for the key and lost my balance, slamming down hard onto the driveway. "Crap!" I sat up and brushed away the small pebbles sticking to my hands. I dumped my purse out onto the pavement; lighters, brush, tampon, change—no key. I stuffed everything back in, trying to remember if I was the last one home and if I might have left the door unlocked.

I stood up and held on to the side of Steve's car, waiting for some semblance of equilibrium. A drop of sweat rolled down my brow and I wiped it away. At least my mom wasn't home yet. I hate having to pretend I'm not trashed.

A warm breeze snaked its way slowly by and I smiled, breathing in the honeysuckle that grew along the driveway. How many years had it been since Lisa and I had pulled the stamens out of hundreds of blossoms for just one drop of nectar? And what had become of us? I spend a great deal of time getting wasted, and Lisa's in rehab.

I leaned back on Steve's car and breathed deep, wanting to remember summer days with Lisa. Things were so easy then.

Oh, God. Coconut.

I sat up, feeling icy cold. I smelled that overpowering coconut lotion that Michael used to wear. The hairs on my arms and neck stood up, my heart pounded. Sickeningly sweet coconut permeated the air.

My head cleared and I bolted for the door. With each breath I drew in that scent, wondering how was it possible? Michael was dead, but I knew without a doubt he was near. Somehow he was out there. In my yard. Close. I fell onto the front door and turned the knob, thanking God it was unlocked. I opened the door and slammed it shut behind me before pulling the deadbolt.

I stood in the entrance hall, breathing in the stale, moist air as I looked into the dark rooms on either side of me. I smelled the two-week-old day lilies rotting in their vase on the entryway table. I smelled the old perfume that clung to my mother's coats in the open closet. No coconut. I counted ten breaths, and then slowly turned back to the front door, squinting out the black windows.

Stupid. Stupid. Stupid. God, I can be so stupid.

Someone probably dropped a bottle of suntan lotion in the street, I thought. Janine probably ran over it. That was the smell. I walked to the door and checked the deadbolt. I peeked out and saw my purse lying in the driveway.

Shit.

Just get a grip and go out and get it, I told myself, but I just stood there frozen. I decided to let my mom bring it in when she and Steve got home. Better to get a talking to about leaving valuables on the ground than to go back outside.

I turned and started up the stairs feeling wobbly again. I went into my room, pulled my shirt off, and flopped onto the bed. My stomach churned from too much wine and ranch dip. Why do I do this? I hate going to bed feeling like I'm going to puke.

The air was so sticky. Sweat trickled down my chest and soaked into my bra. I looked up at the window, still closed. I groaned, remembering the grackles.

Stupid birds! I thought, sitting up. Stupid freaking birds with no purpose but to torment me. Why couldn't bluebirds be nesting in there?

I sat up on my knees and lurched toward the window, fumbling for a grip on the sill. I grunted as I slid the pane up.

Coconut.

"Jordan."

I screamed and rolled off my bed, landing on the floor.

"Help me, Jordan. Let me in."

A dark figure was perched in the branches outside my window. I knew that voice.

Michael.

"Who are you?" I asked, though every part of me already knew the answer.

"It's me, Michael," he moaned. "Help me, Jordan. Please, help me. Let me in."

I slowly pushed myself away from my bed, never taking my gaze away from the dark window. I couldn't see a damn thing, though; it could have been anyone. But I knew it wasn't.

"Michael?" I squeaked out, half hoping this was some kind of joke, because how could Michael be sitting out there in the dark?

"Jordan, help me. Open the window. Let me in."

He sounded so sad, so scared. I wondered if it had all been a mistake, the newspaper articles about Michael's suicide, how they found his body with his throat cut? But how could it be? There'd been a huge investigation; all the local news channels had covered it. They thought he'd been murdered at first, but then there was no sign of a struggle, no other footprints, no other fingerprints on the knife.

I stood up slowly, rubbing the rug fibers off my sweaty arms. Part of me wanted to go to Michael, and part of me was terrified he'd come crashing through my screen.

"What is going on, Michael?" my voice rasped out. "Everyone thinks you're dead. They had your goddamned funeral today!" I took a step toward my bed, trying to get a look at him. Was he a ghost?

"Why weren't you there, Jordan? Why weren't you at my funeral? I stood outside my house tonight. I couldn't sense you. You were never there. I went to my house to see if you were at the party they were throwing. I'm fucking dead and my parents break out the chips and soda for all my friends! But not you; everyone but you."

Then he started to cry. I couldn't believe it. Somehow Michael Green was sitting outside my window. Michael Green was sitting in my tree crying like a baby. My head was spinning.

"Michael, I'm sorry, but . . . what happened to you? How can you be here?"

"This thing attacked me, Jo," he sobbed. "It jumped me from behind. Out of nowhere this thing comes flying at me. I couldn't fight it off, it was so strong. So strong. It cut my throat before I knew what was happening. . . ."

Michael started sobbing again. My eyes felt wide and dry, and I forced myself to blink.

"It was laughing, drinking the blood pouring from my neck, and I couldn't move. It held me in its arms just lapping it all up. I wanted to scream and puke but the fucking thing cut my neck. Do you know what it's like feeling your lungs fill up with blood and not being able to scream?"

I stepped back until I brushed against the wall. It felt cool on my skin, and I wished I were farther away from the window. I wanted to be very far away, not listening to this. I wanted to scream at him to get away from me, from my window, but I just stood there wishing this were all a nightmare. Knowing it wasn't.

"Jordan, let me in. I'm so cold."

"Michael," I whispered. "I can't believe this. It's not possible."

"Let me in," he growled, "and you can feel the scar on my throat. It's thick and white and I catch myself rubbing it. I rub it and pinch the skin with my fingers wondering how my neck put itself back together. And my body doesn't work like it used to, Jordan. Sometimes I start breaking apart, turning to mist or fog or whatever, and have to use every fucking ounce of energy I have to stay in one piece. Let me in and you can see! Help me figure out what I am."

"But they said you were cremated," I said, trying to shoot down this whole crazy story. "They were going to bury your ashes today."

"Yeah," he laughed. "The wonderful, compassionate prick at the funeral home probably filled my urn with kitty litter. I wake up on this slab, and I don't know where the hell I am, and I can barely feel my arms and legs I'm so cold, but I'm happy, see, because I thought I was dead. I don't think I've ever been so happy, and I sit up, and I look around and see where I am, but I'm still happy because I think it's a miracle I survived that lunatic's attack.

"'Hey,' I called out. And I'm so happy my lungs aren't filled with blood, and there is actual sound coming out of my mouth. 'Hey, there's been some sort of mistake.'

"And you know what? The guy isn't so happy to see me. He's not looking at me like it's a miracle; he's looking over at me like I'm a piece of shit. 'Damn,' he says, 'I had a feeling about you; I should have been prepared for this.' And then he looks around all wild like, and grabs this huge needle and starts waving it at me, pointing to this door with his other hand. 'Get out!' he says. 'I won't deal with your kind. Get out of here and do everyone a favor by getting the hell away from here.'"

Michael was crying again, and I realized I was rubbing my skin raw rocking back and forth against the grit my mom had put in the paint to give the walls some texture.

"But then," Michael continued, "I don't move or anything, 'cause I don't understand what's going on, and the son of a bitch lunges at me with the needle. 'Get out of here!' he screams, so I jump off the table, but my legs aren't working real good, and I wipe out on the floor. I'm lying there naked and the son of a bitch kicks me, screaming at me to get out. So I did. And I came to you, Jordan. I knew out of everyone you'd be the one to help me."

"But I can't," I stammered. "I don't know how."

"Don't let me down again, Jo. I don't think I could take it if you let me down again. You owe me. But you have to open the window. You have to ask me in."

Then it clicked. The blood, the invitation.

I'd seen enough horror movies to know why Michael didn't come crashing through my window. I knew he'd figured it out, too, and I sure as hell wasn't going to invite a vampire in; the idea was absolutely ludicrous. It was a death wish.

I have to laugh now—I was so sure I'd never let him in. But how many times have I played out the scenario in my mind since that first night? How many times have I imagined opening my window and letting Michael take me away from all the crap in my life? And how many times have I sat on my mother's bed, slowly shaking a bottle of Valium back and forth, staring at the little pills as they *clicked* and *clacked* in their brown container, thinking how nice it would be to just sleep and not have to deal with anything.

It really wasn't such a ludicrous idea after all.

CHAPTER SIX

I take my seat behind Paul Grubick, whose six-foot-something frame makes an excellent cover when I don't feel like contributing to the class discussion, and I can avoid making eye contact with Danny when he shows up. I have to be careful because, as much as I'd like to take Janine's word that Danny's still interested in me, Janine is famous for reading too much into things, and I don't want to humiliate myself.

Mr. Pappas walks in and slaps a stack of papers on his desk. "People, you disappoint me." He's shaking his head, frowning at the essays we handed in last week. "You're supposed to be the best and the brightest in the school, yet I find myself holding a plethora of papers filled with banal insights and shaky grammar. And might

I remind some of you that not liking *Pilgrim at Tinker Creek* does not give you a free pass for marginal work."

I exhale, thinking my paper's okay. I thought the book was cool. I liked the way the author spent all this time alone hanging out with nature and avoiding all the nonsense that comes from living with people.

When I read it a month ago, I actually fantasized about Michael and me running away from this suburban hellhole to the wilds of Canada. The book takes place down south, but I thought Canada sounded more remote. I even pictured some English class reading my book about it someday: *A Year in the Yukon with Michael!*"

It was a short-lived fantasy, though. The night I asked Michael what he'd think about living in a rustic cabin by a stream or lake, he said it sounded like a total snooze fest—worse than sitting through a musical. Seeing as vampires can't cross running water or swim, lakeside living was probably a bad idea, anyway.

Mr. Pappas looks up at the ceiling, spots a pencil hanging in the acoustic tiles, and hops up on his desk to pull it loose. "I've never understood the appeal of lodging a pencil into the ceiling," he says, jumping down. "Ah, the *machinations* of a bored mind. And I hope you all remember that 'machination' will be on next week's vocabulary test."

He checks out the people heading in late. "Mr. Douglas? Definition please!"

I peek around Paul Grubrick and see Danny walking in with Sara LaRue. Sara hurries to her seat, looking immensely relieved that she didn't get called on.

"Uh, definition?" Danny asks.

Mr. Pappas looks up at him with his eyebrows raised. "Yes, Mr. Douglas, the word is 'machination.'"

"Uh—uh—okay," he stutters. He has the cutest way of stuttering when he's nervous. "Machination, a scheme or plot for, uh, an evil end."

"Very good, Mr. Douglas. Now, take your seat and try to be on time tomorrow."

Danny starts shuffling to his desk, then pauses. "Uh, actually, Mr. Pappas, unless someone intended the pencil to fall out and injure someone, I'd say stuffing it into the ceiling tiles is more an act of stupidity."

The class laughs, and Mr. Pappas smiles. Nobody has to worry he's going to get mad at being corrected, like some teachers would. Mr. Pappas isn't like that. "I have to agree with you, Mr. Douglas. Truth be told, I just couldn't think of a better segue into our next two books—plays, actually. We'll be leaving Thoreau and Ms. Dillard behind to examine the inner workings of some troubled minds." Mr. Pappas places the pencil on his desk and points to a stack of books on the windowsill. "Mr. Douglas, why don't you and Miss Shaw pass out *Hedda Gabler* and *Othello* while I hand out these papers. I've noted on a few of these that a rewrite is required, and one of you will find a note suggesting that he actually read Ms. Dillard's book."

A collective groan goes out as Mr. Pappas starts making the rounds.

I watch Danny walk to the windowsill and grab a

pile of books. He's really tall, basketball tall, and really gawky when he walks. The basketball coach used to harass him about joining the team freshman year, until he saw Danny shoot hoops in gym class. But when he's running he's amazing to watch. All his muscles just click and start working right.

Mr. Pappas clears his throat and I look up. He shakes his head and frowns as he leaves my paper upside down and moves on. What now? I glance sideways at Gina Naples, but she's too engrossed reading the comments on her paper to care about mine.

I flip it over and start to shake. There's no grade. None. Just a big red "SEE ME" scrawled across the top. What the hell does that mean?

I start reading my paper trying to figure out what's wrong.

"Heads up!" Danny drops *Hedda Gabler* on my desk and smiles at me. "Miss you at practice. Uh, Coach is trying to get a winter track thing going, you should, uh, try out for it."

"Yeah, maybe," I mumble, my cheeks firing up.

Miss you? Does he mean he misses me, or the team misses me? What does he mean? I wonder if it *is* possible to implode?

I turn back and watch him hand out a few plays, and wish I could've gone out for the cross-country team. I remember when he started running with me at practice. Man, I had to hustle to keep up with his long legs. Then he started sitting with me on the bus rides to our meets, and one time we found this really cool moth stuck against the side of the bus, and I told him I had a thing for insects, which is not something I've shared with a lot of people. I discovered early on that most people do not find insects as fascinating as I do. Most people find insects repulsive, and when they find out you have a thing for six legged critters, they find you repulsive as well.

But I got brave and told him about the hissing cockroaches I used to have. My dad sent them to me from South Carolina when I was ten. My mom freaked. "Your father's sitting in some fancy beach house and sends giant bugs to my home. Who the hell does he think he is!" But I got to keep them because she didn't want to give him the satisfaction of knowing it pissed her off. I sometimes think the only reason he sent them was to get to her.

But they were so cool; these huge, fat, shiny cockroaches that hissed when I picked them up. Lisa even got used to them, and one day we put them in the tub just before her brother was going to take a shower. We laughed our asses off when her soccer star brother screamed like a girl over a few roaches in the tub.

When the last one died, my dad said he'd send some more, but he never did. I guess he figured it wasn't worth the hassle if my mom wasn't put out.

But Danny didn't look at me like I was some nut job for having cockroaches as pets. He got all excited and told me about the ant farms he'd had all over his room when he was a kid. He'd had nine of them connected with plastic tubing. And it turned out we'd both read this ant book by this Cornell University guy. We were in some sort of geek heaven on those bus rides. I'd even stopped mooning over Michael. All I was thinking about was Danny, wondering when he was going to make the move I was sure he was going to make.

He finally did at the end of the year track party at Melissa Smith's house. It was different from the usual parties I go to: no booze, no smokes, just barbeque and soda. I didn't really want to go because I couldn't remember being at a party without being wasted. Well, not since seventh grade, anyway, and I really didn't hang out with anyone on the team outside of practice. But I knew Danny was going to be there, and if nothing happened that night, I would have to wait until school started again to talk to him.

The party was actually fun, and I realized how nice it was conversing with people who were of sound mind and unaltered states. I almost started thinking this could be a new thing for me. Sobriety.

A bunch of us were hanging out in a gazebo, and somehow Danny and I had managed to sit next to each other. I needed to go to the bathroom, but I didn't want to lose my spot. Finally the crowd started to thin out as people got up to get a soda or go swimming, and it was just Danny and me sitting under these small twinkling lights. It was so nice being with him, talking about books we'd read and bands we liked. And then he just leaned in and kissed me.

God, my heart was pounding. Then about half the team came running up the steps, talking and laughing.

I looked up at his face, at his big gray eyes, and felt so light and so good. We just sat there holding hands until his mom came and picked him up.

He called me after that and left three messages, and maybe if I'd been home any one of those times and answered the phone, everything would be different now. I wanted it to be different, because since Michael and I broke up, all I'd had were a bunch of what Rachael calls "flybys." And I hate the flybys: guys I start making out with at a party just because every once in a while I need some human contact. I need to feel like someone's noticed me.

But it always goes further than I want. I want to say stop, but it's just easier to go with the flow, go all the way. It's just easier not to return the phone calls from the ones hoping for a repeat performance.

But Danny was different, and I blew it. I was too scared to return his calls, another charming facet of my social anxiety disorder. I panic thinking someone's mom or older sister will answer the phone and I won't know what to say. I figured we had the whole summer ahead of us, but then Michael came calling and summer was over.

I turn around and look at Danny. Damn! He's at his desk smiling at me. I whip my head back to the front.

I never told Michael about the cockroaches.

"Interested?" Marnie Shaw is staring down at me, waving a copy of *Othello*.

How long has she been standing there? My cheeks feel like embers.

"He's taken." She smirks. "He was all gropey in the hall with Sara, that's why they were late."

Taken? Sara? When did that happen? I am going to kill Janine!

I reach out and Marnie hands me the book. "Better luck next time," she says, and moves on.

At least Michael wants me. At least Michael didn't give up on me.

I am so twisted.

When the bell rings, I jump out of my seat. I want to get out of the class as soon as possible. I don't want to think about Danny, and I don't want to talk to Mr. Pappas about my paper. I don't give a damn about my paper.

"Jordan, I'd like to speak to you," Mr. Pappas calls out.

Great! I take a deep breath, turn around, and push my way past the kids heading out the door. My cheeks are burning again.

"Have a seat," he says as he closes the door.

"I have French class second period," I say, hating how my voice came out several octaves too high.

"Actually I talked with Ms. Chubb, and she thought what we had to talk about was worth missing a bit of class."

So I sit, clutching my binder to keep from visibly shaking. What is going on?

Mr. Pappas sits on the front of his desk and smiles at me. I know he is trying to put me at ease, but he must see that I'm about to lose it any second now. Why can't he leave me alone?

"Jordan, I've noticed something about the two papers you've handed in. Each time they were due, you were absent the day before. No big deal, perhaps, but I wanted you to know that I noticed. You wouldn't be the first student to cut school to write a paper that was due the next day, but I don't want it to become a habit. It's your job to manage your time wisely."

He's pausing like I'm supposed to jump in and say something, but I can't open my mouth, because if I do I know I'll start crying. God, I wish I was one of those kids who gives off that I-couldn't-give-a-crap-what-you-teachers-think-of-me vibe. And why does he care if I take a day off to write a paper? My mother doesn't care; she just writes whatever stupid note I ask her to. She never even questions why she's writing them.

"And I want you to know I've spoken to a few of your teachers from this year and last and we are all concerned about your erratic school performance and absences. You seem to miss a lot of your afternoon classes, especially Friday afternoon ones."

He's laughing a bit, like he's in on some big joke.

"I handed in notes," I squeak out. "My mom knows." I immediately regret saying that as his smile dissolves. No more big joke.

"Yes, I'm aware of the notes," he says, his serious look punctuated with a big sigh.

He leans forward, and I wish I could back away. "Do we really need to get your mother in here and have her account for all those dental appointments and stomach aches? How many notes do you think she'll write after she's called in to speak to Dr. Deluca?" He opens a folder perched on his knees. "Do you think your mother is aware that she excused *nineteen* of your absences in Mr. Bell's class last year? That's one day short of an automatic failure, but I'm sure you know that. I'm sure you kept a very accurate count."

That did it. Now the tears are coming. I look down, knowing it's hopeless to try to hide them. Mr. Pappas gets up and returns with a box of tissues. I hate him for doing this to me. I reach out and grab one, and blot my face, never taking my eyes off the crooked heart someone must have spent an entire semester carving into the desk.

"Jordan, I didn't mean to upset you. I'm just concerned; all of us are concerned. You're a bright girl who seems to be very cavalier about her future. Now, I've talked to Mrs. Verona and—"

"Oh, God," I murmur. I can't help it, that woman is the biggest idiot in this school, with all her "I'm here for you kids" crap.

"Look, I know some of you think the guidance counselors are a bit of a joke, but Mrs. Verona has helped a lot of students. Nobody is going to make you see her; we just think you seem a bit in over your head."

Over my head, huh? Maybe Mr. Pappas and Mrs. Verona can pull their little straight talk routine with Michael and get him the hell out of my tree, get my mother out of the mall, and get my father to call when it's not my birthday.

"We just don't want to see you fall through the cracks, Jordan."

Too late. I'm quite comfortable in here, thank you very much.

Silence. Big, awkward silence. Well, except for the disgusting sound of mucous being sucked back into my sinuses.

"Just think about what I've said, Jordan. And . . ."

Gee, suddenly Mr. Pappas is at a loss for words. What did he think I was going to do, thank him for pointing out what a mess I am? Like I didn't know?

"Look, take as much time as you need, Jordan. And don't worry about French class."

"Isn't that cutting?" I hiss, running my finger over the heart.

He sighs again. I guess he was hoping for more breakthough and less bitterness. "We're here if you need us," he says, and walks out of the classroom, shutting the door quietly behind him.

I take my mirror out of my purse. Big red nose, red-rimmed eyes—just lovely. I'd laugh if I wasn't so screwed. How does Mr. Pappas expect me to walk around with a huge red nose and blotchy face? What if Danny sees me like this? What if Danny and Sara see me?

I'm suddenly aware of the clock ticking on the wall. The second hand is stuck on the number ten; it's been stuck there all semester and nobody's bothered to fix it. The clicking noise is driving me insane, and I can't exactly go to Mrs. Chubb's class looking like a freak, so I decide to go home. Just let them call my mother in; I'd love to hear her try to explain all those notes to Dr. Deluca. It would serve her right.

I blow my nose and check the mirror one more time. Definitely time to go home. I peek out into the halls and head for the science wing, where there's never anyone watching the exits. I round the corner, picking up speed, hoping to avoid any teachers.

"Jordan!"

I turn and see Lisa. How bad is this day going to get? I tip my chin down, trying to hide my face under my hair. "Hey, Lisa."

"Are you okay?"

"Yeah, but I've got to go home. Good to see you." I start walking, hoping she'll let me go.

"Jordan, wait."

I stop and face her. When Lisa and I were friends, she'd always laugh about how the littlest things would bring me to tears. *Be strong, be cool, and never let them see you cry,* she'd say. I'm painfully aware of how awful I look but decide to cop a "be cool" attitude so Lisa won't be shaking her head, thinking, "same old Jordan."

"When did you get home?" I ask, looking her in the eyes. I notice that Lisa isn't looking so hot, either. She's got a red rash covering her cheeks and nose.

"Last weekend. This is my first day back." She tilts her head to the side and scans the posters on the wall. "Um, are you sure you're okay? You look . . ."

I smile, concentrating hard to make it seem natural. "I'm fine; it's allergies. That's why I'm heading home. Gotta get some meds."

"Oh, well. Okay. If you want to talk, you can call me. You know that, right?"

"Yeah, you too, Lisa. Give me a call if you need anything. Well, I really need to get that Clarinex! See you."

I wave and head out the door. A cold breeze slaps me as my head drops and my shoulders cave in.

I can't wait to see Michael tonight.

CHAPTER SEVEN

God, where is he? I will beg him to put me out of my misery. None of this we-can-be-together-for-all-eternity crap! I don't want to even think about tomorrow. I just want my room to stop spinning and my stomach to stop heaving.

It gets dark so early now, and next week will be daylight savings time. It'll be dark at five freaking o'clock, and Michael could be anywhere. I can't stay after school and join the track team, it's too dark! I can't hang out on the weekends 'cause it's too dark. It's too damn dark and Michael Green's got me on a curfew.

I squint at my clock: 12:41.

Where the hell is he? I am so sick of this—so sick of waiting for Michael.

He has a whole school to choose from, why did he pick me to haunt? We were together for two months. Why the hell is he so bent on spending his whole stupid unnatural life with me? I hate him! I hate Michael Green!

God, why did I brush my teeth? The mint and smoke and rum are mingling in my mouth in the most disgusting way. I need to take deep, slow breaths so I won't throw up.

Rum sucks.

Michael sucks.

Would Michael even want me this way? Would all the crap in my blood make *him* sick? Ha! That would be great. I'll open the window and invite him in—the moment he's been waiting for. He'll put his mouth on the soft part of my neck he loved to kiss, his teeth will pierce my skin, and my blood will be poison.

Yeah, that would be great.

I sit up and sway in my bed, running my fingers back and forth over the screen. I wonder if Michael will hear the noise and come to me. Hard to believe this flimsy little bit of wire mesh is all that stands between Michael and me. I open the window some more.

Maybe tonight's the night.

I breathe in the cool air and whisper, "Michael, where are you?"

I need to talk to you. I need to know why you chose me. We were together so long ago. For as long as a heartbeat when you think of the time that's passed since I was yours.

I fall back onto my pillow with a thump. I need to

puke, and I need to know why Michael Green comes to me, begging *me* to let him in.

I remember driving around in Michael's car. We'd pull over at the beach, park under the trees at the back of the lot, and crack the windows to smell the hot, salty air. We never said much, we'd just hit the backseat with a pack of condoms and steam up the already warm night. I replay that summer, trying to figure out what we did that might have made a deep impression on Michael—something special that makes him come to my window every night.

"Jordan, let me in."

His words erase the summer nights, and I realize I'm shaking. I want to reach out and touch the screen, to touch Michael and feel how cold he really is.

"Ah, Michael. So nizze of you t'drop by." I hear the words leaving my mouth in a sloppy, jumbled slur. "What have you been doing this very fine evening?" I ask, slowly, carefully moving my lips and tongue, trying to keep my words from blending together.

"Are you drunk again, Jo?"

I decide to ignore his question. He knows the answer.

"I've been thinking about our relationship, Michael. There'z a whole lot I don't know about the *new you*! Now what kind of friend does that make me? A shitty one! So let'z talk about you, Michael. What do you do before our little nocturnal tête-à-têtes? How do you fill your time before you skulk outside my window?"

"God, you're trashed."

"Now, now. We're going to talk about *you*! Besides, you are a very big part of the reason I felt compelled to chug quite a bit of a very nasty bottle of rum."

"Maybe I should go. I can't talk to you when you're like this."

I wait for him to jump from the tree, but he stays. I clutch my stomach and wonder if I should make myself throw up. The way Rachael tells it, any bulimic middle schooler can do it; I just need to work on my finger placement in the back of my throat.

But I have things I want to say to Michael, and vomiting would most definitely spoil the mood.

"You know, if you had shown up a little earlier, I might have met you outside in the tree. I finally decided I was too faced to get through the branches. Didn't want you to find me with a broken neck at the bottom of the tree, though I considered that option."

I wait for the laugh, but apparently becoming a vampire has destroyed what little sense of humor Michael had.

"Anyway, I got to thinking about you and what it is you do, and I want to know what I'd be getting myself into. You come to me every night, sitting in that damn tree, asking me to let you in, but what will happen? Will we run around together like Heathcliff and Catherine? Except instead of slitting people's throats on the moors, we'll be hunting them down in the parking garage at the mall? Is that what we'd do?"

Now Michael laughs, like it's such a ridiculous notion: him slitting people's throats. But it's a nervous laugh, and I don't think he's feeling very sure of himself. I bet he's desperately trying to make that jock brain of his figure out the right answer—the answer that will get me to open the window. And I bet he's desperately trying to figure out who the hell Heathcliff is.

"I haven't killed anyone, I—I wouldn't do that. You don't have to do that. Just know it isn't bad. And we'd be together."

"Just know it isn't bad? That'z too funny! You drink blood, for God's sake. I think we need to be up-front about that. I'm feeling pretty shitty about things today, and if you want that invite, you'd better try damn hard to make it seem appetizing!"

"Why are you talking like this? Did something happen today?"

Oh, God. Is that pity in his voice? I think I must have hit rock bottom to elicit pity from someone who's been dead for three months.

"I'm just sick of everything. Sick of you. Why are you here, Michael? Why are you doing this to me?"

"I love you," he whispers.

"You're so full of shit," I spit. "We were together for sixty-three days, over a year ago. It took you all of two seconds to get over me. Why are you really here?"

"Hey, aren't you forgetting that *you* broke up with *me*, Jo? First day of school and you just break it off. 'This just isn't going to work. We're too different.' That's all you said. What was I supposed to do?"

I hear Michael tearing the dry leaves off the tree and crunching them between his fingers. I want to tell him it was all a mistake—that I just snapped, that I was scared.

"Why did you do it, Jo? I thought we belonged together. God, you were so easy to talk to. I could tell you anything. I could be someone different with you. But then you dumped me. And it wasn't even for someone else. I racked my brain for months trying to figure out what I missed, because I thought everything was great. You ripped my heart out, and you never told me why. You never told me what'd I'd done that made you stop loving me."

How can I explain this to someone like Michael?

Michael walked in the world looking everyone straight in the eye. He thrived on human contact. So how could Michael understand that I go to school every day with my stomach in a knot because, in seventeen years on this planet, I haven't figured out how to make small talk, or even just say hello to people without feeling like an idiot. He'd never understand. He's just not made that way.

And that first day of school totally threw me. When we pulled into the parking lot, I was still in my stupid summer-love mode, still under Michael's magic spell, feeling calm and confident, thinking I could face this year, maybe even walk down the halls and look people in the eye as long as I was on Michael's arm.

Then we got out of his car, and kids I've known since first grade, kids who have barely looked my way in years, are swarming all over us.

"Michael, what period do you have lunch?"

"Michael, are you in Mr. Nucci's chem class with me?"

"Michael, why didn't you call me back?"

"Michael, you're coming to my party this weekend, right?"

Michael's lived in this town for two months and without my knowing it, he's somehow reached the highest stratosphere of the student body.

I mean, I knew he played baseball in the summer league, and he said he was doing really well at football practice, but I never would have guessed that the whole school had noticed. I supposed I should have gone to his games or practice or something. Then at least I would've had some warning, but I had to babysit the twins. Honestly, I was relieved I didn't have to go. Sitting in the bleachers yelling "Go, team!" isn't really my thing. But Michael, he never said a word. You'd think he would have had something to say about being discovered by the school's upper crust! I felt like an idiot. I wondered if they knew we were even going out?

First period was a blur. I ignored Mr. Nucci's lecture on the dedication he expected of his AP chem students and had a lengthy discussion with myself as to whether or not I could seamlessly fit in with the in crowd. Being Michael's girlfriend was my ticket to the front tables by the windows that overlook the courtyard. For once I could sit and watch the kids go by. I could whisper and giggle and watch my reflection in the glass as I flipped my hair. I imagined bringing Rachael along. Well, after she had dumped her fishnets and high-heeled boots for something a little more mainstream, and finished growing out her Mohawk, and stopped talking about orgasms all the time.

I could be friends with Lisa again.

By the end of second-period gym class, I'd almost convinced myself that it was possible. I was actually starting to breathe normally. I was feeling good and I didn't even care that I was changing out of my shorts in front of everyone, when Marnie Shaw, the Mouth, sauntered over, wearing nothing but a bright pink thong.

"Congratulations, Jordan," she said, smiling at me like we'd been friends so long I wouldn't turn beet red seeing her parade around practically naked. "I hear you're going out with Michael Green. You'll have to sit with us at lunch and tell us all about it!"

Sit with us at lunch? I almost puked right then. But instead of tossing my breakfast all over her bare feet, I snapped. I mean, I may have fantasized about being popular, but I don't think I ever really wanted to be. God, the maintenance involved would be overwhelming. Too much smiling, too much attention to clothes, too much worry. I had a hard enough time figuring out the people who liked me, let alone negotiating life around the Mouth and her friends.

In a split second that fight-or-flight reaction sent crazy amounts of adrenaline surging through my body, and it was good-bye summer love. Michael and I weren't the cozy little team I had envisioned. Michael and I were a mistake that nobody had noticed until school started. Well, school was in session and I'd had my reality check.

"No," I stammered. "We're not."

Marnie nodded knowingly, like she hadn't believed it was true. "Oh, I guess I heard wrong."

She turned and I watched her tan ass saunter away. *That looks like it hurts,* I thought numbly.

I tuned out the whispering, the laughter, and the other locker-room talk, and rehearsed what I would say to Michael.

I remember how cold the lock felt as I snapped it shut before I headed out. I left the locker room and went to Mrs. Verona's office. "That AP chem class is going to be more work than I thought," I told her.

Mrs. Verona frowned. "But you're on the AP track, Jordan, and your teachers felt this was the right spot for you, despite your uneven work in the past. I think dropping it would be a big mistake."

I shook my head. "No, I'm sure," I said.

"Well, I would advise giving it at least a full week, but if you're determined to do it, have a parent sign the form and leave it in the box outside my door. You'll need to sign up for the other section, as well." She shut my folder and looked up at me. "And Jordan, if you ever want to talk, I'm here for you."

So I dropped AP chem and I dumped Michael.

I regretted the latter decision for the next ten months. Ten months of wondering why I was such an idiot. Ten months of watching Michael go on like that summer never happened. I wanted to take it all back. I wanted Michael back. I wanted him to beg me to take him back. I would even wear thongs and sit at the tables by the courtyard if Michael would just take me back.

But he never asked, and I couldn't tell him that I broke up with him because the sight of Marnie Shaw's breasts set off a panic attack. I couldn't tell him, and worse, he didn't seem to care. The hurt and anger in his eyes was over in a flash. It killed me that Michael could let me go, that he could stop loving me. That he couldn't look at me, look in my eyes and see it was all a mistake. He didn't look back, and later that day he was making out with Marnie's best friend on the fountain.

But maybe he loved me all that time, like I loved him.

Maybe he watched me and he felt as helpless as I did. Maybe he didn't know how to fix it, either. Maybe once I said those words, once I told him we were too different, he started doubting those two months, doubting whether it was all real.

Did I do that to Michael? Did I make him doubt that I loved him?

I turn to the window and feel my stomach roil. I swallow back the bile rising in my throat. "Michael, let me see your face. I need to see your eyes."

"Jordan, just open the window. You know I love you. I never stopped loving you. Just let me in. Open the window and let me get warm. Let me in and we can be together again. Let me in so I can love you again."

"I love you, too, but I need to see your face, Michael. I need to see it's still you."

"Just let me in. Please, please, let me in."

I hear his voice hiss with urgency; his words ring in my ears. My hand reaches out toward the bottom of the window and I can't stop it. I don't know if I want to stop it.

"Open it. Open it. Open it. Do it, Jo. Keep going," he whispers frantically as my fingers catch the bottom of the sill.

I want to think clearly, but his voice is fogging my head. My fingers trace the sill back and forth, and I can't stop them.

"Keep going, we're so close now. But you need to ask me in. Ask me in."

His voice is getting louder, edgier.

"You can't go on like this, Jo. I can stop it all, and we'll be together again."

My body shakes as the sobs heave my chest up and down. I want to open the window. I want to, but I'm so scared.

"Ask me in and I'll open it for you. Just say the words and I'll come in and take care of you."

My heart is beating wildly and I can't unlock my fingers from the sill. I want to pull them back, to think this through, but Michael's words are pounding in my head—controlling my hands, urging me on.

"Remember how easy it was, Jo? Remember when it was just you and me? You've got to want that again. I know you do. Ask me in!"

God, I want things to be easy again. I want to stop worrying about everything. I want someone to take care of me. I want Michael to take care of me. I pull myself up to the window and push it all the way up, amazed it slides so easily in the frame.

"Oh, yes," he hisses. "Do it, now!"

My eyes get wide and I hear myself gasp. His voice is different now. It's hard. Hungry.

My heart triple beats and my head clears a bit. I'm not so sure now.

I fumble with the screen, wishing I could make myself stop. I want to stop; a voice in my head is telling me this isn't what I really want.

My knuckles scrape roughly against the wire mesh; I pull my hand back, feeling the blood well up in the tiny scratches. I hear Michael moan; he must smell the blood. I stop searching for the latch and collapse against the screen, tears streaming down my face.

"No, don't stop! Damn it! Don't stop!" he screams.

"I need to see your face!"

My wet cheek is flat against the screen, and Michael leans in and presses his mouth on the other side.

"Jo, please."

His wintry lips sting my cheek through the mesh. The smell of coconut and something dark and wet, like damp earth, fills my head. I breathe in Michael's new smell and gag as dinner comes racing up in my throat. I scramble out of bed and trip and stumble my way to the bathroom, where I empty my stomach.

The toilet feels like ice. I wish I could stop crying

and spitting into the bowl. I want to wipe the sweat from my lip, but I'm afraid I'll get sick again if I move. Why is everything so cold?

My stomach finally stops heaving. I reach out and grab a towel, pulling it to the floor and pushing it under my head. I pull another towel down and wrap it around my shoulders. I curl up into a ball, wondering if I will remember almost letting Michael in when I wake up.

CHAPTER EIGHT

I'm lying on the bathroom floor, trying to decide if I should get up. The doorbell is ringing and I wonder if my mom is still home. What time is it, anyway?

Feet are pounding up the stairs. I sit up and the dull throb in my head gets worse.

"Yoooo-hooo! Jordan? Where are you?"

It's Gabby. Janine is probably here, too.

"Where is she?"

"Check her bathroom."

"Go away," I call out hoarsely. I sound like crap.

"What's the matter? Is someone not feeling so good?" Gabby sings brightly from the other side of the door.

"I'm shutting the window, it's cold as hell in here," Janine says.

I hear my window close and rub my knuckles over my lips, feeling the small scabs and bits of skin sticking out from where I scraped my hand against the screen. The cuts are still raw and I shake my head as I remember last night. Where would I be right now if I had gotten that screen open? *What* would I be?

I want to tell them to nail my window shut so I won't be tempted to let Michael in again.

My toes are like ten little icicles; I push the towel down to cover my feet.

"Should we check on her?" Janine says.

"Give her a minute."

I hear someone else jog up the stairs. I hope it's not my mom.

"Look under the bed," Rachael says, coming into my room. "Let's see what made Miss America toss her cookies!"

Apparently Rachael has made up with Gabby and Janine.

"Your mom heard you throwing up last night," she continues, "and according to the note she left, she would have checked on you if she wasn't having 'the worst migraine imaginable.' She really thought she was going to die this time. Classic self-absorption!"

"Well, that would be, what, the fifth time this year she was close to death?" Gabby asks. "I can just hear her. 'Oh my . . . God, I thought this was the one! I thought my head would split open right there on my pillow. Gee, I hope Jordan's okay. I think I heard her puking her guts out last night. I'd check to see if she's still alive, but I have to get to a christening!'"

In my mother's defense, I use throwing up as an excuse to get out of school a lot, and she's long past worrying about it. She just keeps telling me I need to wash my hands more often to avoid picking up whatever's going around. She's never figured out it has more to do with booze and/or faking it than poor hygiene.

"Well, looky what I found!"

I hear Rachael's muffled voice. She must be half under my bed, fishing out the bottle from behind all the clothes and books.

"Survey says: rum! And it's almost empty. I sure as hell hope you didn't drink all of that last night."

"Holy shit!" Janine says. "No wonder she freakin' puked."

I stare blankly at the ceiling. Small specks of mold are growing, and I wonder if I need to worry about them. I think I read breathing mold is dangerous.

"It wasn't the rum," I call out. "It's this mold growing in here. I'll be better once I get some fresh air. Why don't you let me get myself together and I'll call you later."

They're laughing now. Someone is wondering if you can get high if you breathe in mold, though I'm not sure if it's Rachael of Gabby. I hear my drawers opening.

"Let's find you something to wear tonight," Rachael says.

I get up slowly and sit on the toilet; I'm surprised I don't feel too terrible. "Look, guys, give me a chance to wake up and I promise I'll call you tonight."

Rachael laughs. "No way! We're not leaving until you come out. I've examined your case and decided you're suffering from agoraphobia. We've come for an intervention."

"And the party," Gabby adds. "You said you'd go to Mark Menducci's party. His dad got this new isolation tank, too. I used it at the last one and it's incredible. Smoke a joint, get in, and you'll be right with the world."

"Oh, yeah. It's totally freaky!" Janine squeals. "And it's even better if you go in with someone else."

Go into an isolation tank with somebody?

I manage to stand up. I'm figuring it's pretty late in the day because, other than the headache, I feel pretty good. I guess I've had plenty of time to sleep it off.

I wish they'd just leave, though. There's no way I'm going to the party tonight. Besides the fact that I'd have to worry about Michael, I have no intention of going anywhere I'll have to watch Danny and Sara together.

"I can't go; I wasn't invited." I'm never invited. I just go with Gabby; she knows everyone and gets invited everywhere. Well, at least with our group. I'm always afraid I'll get to the door and they'll let her in but not me. It never happens, but for once it would be nice to be personally invited.

"You weren't invited because you're a hermit and you never talk to anyone, but Mark said you could come." Gabby says.

"Yeah," Janine adds. "Now, like, get your butt out of the bathroom and let us intervent you!"

Gabby laughs. "You can't *intervent* someone, you idiot. You have an intervention on someone's behalf!"

"Excuse me, Einstein. Sorry I'm not taking freakin' advanced English classes like the rest of you."

"Janine," Gabby says, "we love you even though you'll never get more than a two hundred on the verbal SAT."

I splash some cold water on my face and decide to leave the bathroom before Janine threatens to stop driving us around anymore. Whenever Gabby starts making fun of her IQ, it's the first thing Janine does. And where would we be without her car?

I open the door and roll my eyes. The three of them are sitting on my bed, looking very serious. I sit at my desk chair and swivel it around to face them. "Intervent away."

Janine glares at Gabby. "See, it is a word."

"Is not!" Gabby turns to me. "What happened to you yesterday, by the way?"

"Mr. Pappas took me to task for taking one of my 'day before the paper's due' days off."

Rachael snorts. "It's about time someone busted you for those. It's totally unhealthy the way your mom writes you whatever the hell excuse you need. Maybe now you can break away from that weird codependence stuff you two have going on."

"Yeah, well, Mr. Pappas agrees with you, and he also nailed me for cutting classes."

Rachael throws herself back onto my bed. "Hmmm! Maybe I should start misbehaving, I'd love Mr. Pappas to nail me!"

Janine shudders. "Ew, he's like, so old. He has no hair!"

"I'm attracted to his intellect," Rachael says, getting up to sift through my closet.

"So where were you after he talked to you?" Janine asks.

Gabby starts bouncing on my bed, raising her hand. "Ooooh! Ooooh! I know. You crumbled under the pressure and cut out of school. Then you raided the liquor cabinet, watched soap operas and inane talk shows where the half-naked guests have to be restrained from killing each other, smoked a few joints, and got royally sick."

I nod, and Gabby looks very proud of herself. I have to hand it to her; she really does know her stuff.

"So, what's the deal, Jordie-pie? Are you coming to Mark's willingly, or do we have to take you there by force?"

Honestly, I don't know what to say. It would be such a relief to go out and have fun, but what about Michael? What if he follows me there? If I meet Michael out in the dark, do I have any say in the matter, or am I meat?

"And don't forget that someone special will be there!" Janine adds.

"If you're referring to Danny, I suppose he might be there with his *girlfriend*, Sara."

Rachael takes a sweater out of my closet and smiles slyly. "No, no, no! You've got it all wrong, and if you had stayed at school you'd know that. You still get Track Boy all hot and bothered! He came to our table at lunch yesterday looking for you."

"But I heard he was seeing Sara."

Rachael takes off her shirt, grabs my red sweater off the hanger, and pulls it on over her head. "Seems Danny wanted to talk to you because Gina Naples told him she heard Marnie tell you he was going out with Sara. But, for once, the Mouth was wrong. Sara was only hugging Danny before class because she got an A on a test Danny tutored her for and . . ." Rachael takes a deep breath. "Sara really likes Luke Malloy, and Danny would like to pick up where you two left off at that track party."

I'm positively giddy. "He said that?"

"Well." Rachael laughs. "You told me about sucking face at the track party; I'm just filling in the pieces. But he did say he wanted to set the record straight. And why bother if he wasn't still interested?"

"Why *didn't* you two hook up?" Janine asks. "You were all stoked and then . . . nothing?"

"Michael died," I say quietly.

Gabby starts waving the bottle of rum up in the air like a conductor's baton. "Yeah, so ding-dong, the asshole's dead. What does that have to do with Danny?"

He's not *all* dead, I want to scream. He comes to my window every freakin' night, that's what it has to do with Danny.

Rachael throws a beanie baby at Gabby. "For God's sake, you have the sensitivity of a baboon. You seriously need to learn you *don't* have to say whatever pops into your head!"

Gabby shakes her head and turns to me, looking sympathetic. "Sorry you went out with an asshole."

Rachael scowls. "Don't you have stuff to do?"

"Yeah." Gabby puts the bottle of rum on my bedside table. "Janine and I have to pick up a few party supplies from this new guy who grows his own weed."

"I'm staying here to keep an eye on you," Rachael says. "And you said we could try on dresses."

She smiles, and I suppose the purple-hair crack has been forgotten.

Janine is jingling her car keys and heading for my door. "I told Danny you were going to be at the party. He said he'd try to make it." She throws her keys in the air and catches them with her other hand.

"I think he'd be good for you," Gabby says as she heads out. "He's more your type."

How do you know what my type is? I think. Michael's words echo in my head. *They don't really know you. They don't even care.* I'm about to concede that one to Michael, but then I realize none of them had to show up today. And yeah, Gabby's totally snarky, but they all came over because they *do* care.

Rachael takes off my sweater and puts on her own shirt. She looks at me and shakes her head. "No offense, but we have some serious under-eye makeup work to do." She points to the bathroom.

I push myself off the chair. My stomach is starting to feel queasy. "I need to eat first. Or shower."

"Okay, lets get you fed and shower-fresh. And you should take a few vitamins or something. Your skin is translucent. Good thing Danny is into the natural look."

We head down to the kitchen and I smile, thinking how surprised my mother would be to find out she has more in common with Rachael than she'd suppose. They both want to do me over. Okay, there goes the smile, because now I'm wondering why they both think I'm so pathetic that I can't get by without some change.

Rachael slides up to the breakfast bar while I take out some bagels. "Onion, sesame, or wheat?" I ask.

"Wheat, of course, and I think you'd better stay away from the onion. You'll thank me later when you're with Danny tonight."

I start cutting the bagels in half. "Do you really think he'll show up?"

Rachael laughs. "Do you want him to?"

"I think so."

"Think so?"

"I guess. Okay, yes." I hate to admit it, because if he doesn't show, I'll look like an idiot. I turn to Rachael. She tells me everything about her boyfriends, down to how many orgasms she's had and what her boyfriends' *stuff* tastes like. What do I tell her? Some, just enough to let her feel she's gotten below the surface, but maybe she could be like Lisa. Maybe I've never given her a chance.

I put down the knife and look her in the eye. "Why does everyone think I wasn't Michael's type? I mean, why is it so impossible for everyone to believe that Michael could have liked me?"

Rachael's eyes widen. I guess she wasn't expecting me to switch topics like that. I guess she wasn't expecting me to raise my voice. I think I'm a little surprised, too.

"Jordan, it's not that you weren't *his* type, it was just so obvious he wasn't *your* type. Well, let me correct that; Michael was everybody's type. He was a big stud-boy jerk bursting with testosterone, and he knew it. He knew any female within pheromone-sniffing range would be lusting after him. Hell, I thought more than once about how nice it would be to get a little action from the Green Monster, but I never liked him. There's a difference." She shakes her head.

"But Michael and I had something amazing, something I'm not sure I'll ever have again."

Rachael starts laughing hysterically. So glad I opened myself up to this ridicule.

"Jordan, you will love again," she says dramatically. "Many, many times. I know he was your first, but girl, you have to get over it. He got over it. And I believe you broke up with him, right? That's what you told us, anyway."

"Yes! I did, and I regretted it."

And *he* hasn't gotten over it, thank you!

"Why did you break up with him if he was this love of a lifetime? Be honest, why did you do it?"

"It was Marnie, and the thought of having to hang out with her and her friends."

"Yeah, yeah, the great 'Thong Incident,' but if you really loved him you could have gotten past that." Rachael picks up the saltshaker and pours a pile of salt onto the table. "Did you and Michael really have that much in common? Was he into the stuff you like? 'Cause I never figured Michael to be the bookish type. What *did* you guys talk about after you played Rock, Paper, Scissors to figure out who was going to take a turn lying in the wet spot on the bed?"

She's drawing hearts in the salt; I wish I'd never brought this up. I don't really want to think about this anymore. We were in love, that's all that matters.

"I'm waiting, or can't you think of anything?"

"We had a lot in common. We'd, uh . . ." We'd sit in bed and I'd go into great detail about some book I was reading, or what I'd done with the twins, or how my mom was driving me crazy, and he would nod occasionally, eyes half closed. I assumed he was listening. He'd talk about practice, and keep me up-to-date with Major League Baseball. How much did I listen? Did I really care? What *did* we talk about before he rolled over and we did it again?

"Look, you were doing it with a gorgeous guy and after awhile you realized there was nothing else there.

Happens all the time. You're just having a harder than normal time admitting your virginal dream of marrying the guy that popped your cherry is pure fantasy. You can keep blaming the Mouth, or you can be honest with yourself. You and Michael were all sex with nothing else very deep going on, and the evil pink thong was just a good excuse for breaking up with him."

Better than admitting I was bored with Michael? Better than admitting I gave it up so easily to a guy who immediately replaced me, and went on to sleep with the whole cheerleading squad? How do I face the fact that maybe I've been mooning over Michael all this time because it's better than owning up to the fact that the whole thing was a colossal mistake. That I totally got off on the attention and didn't care who was giving it to me, and that deep down a part of me thought it would be totally cool to sit at the front tables. So I imagined we'd had this undying love, and then believed it was true.

I guess my mother doesn't have an exclusive on the crazies.

"Try this," Rachael says. "When you think of Michael, what is the first word that pops into your head?"

"Regret," I say without hesitating.

"Danny?"

"Regret," I whisper. "A different kind, though."

"Now, how did a summer of bumping uglies with Michael compare to hanging out with Danny down at the track?" Rachael asks.

I turn away from her and put the bagels in the toaster oven. Michael says he loves me. But what about me does he love? He doesn't even know me.

I'm such an idiot, a huge, Titanic-size idiot. God, I almost opened my freakin' window last night! I brace myself against the counter and try to resist the urge to slam my head into the toaster oven.

Rachael walks over and puts an arm around my shoulder. I'm biting my lip, trying not to cry. I want to tell her about Michael. I want her to make Michael disappear, because I do not want to spend an eternity with Michael. I couldn't even make it past sixty-three days with him.

"It's time to let it go and concentrate on the future, on Danny." Rachael reaches past me and pushes down the switch on the toaster. "Works better if you turn it on."

"Michael was kind of thick," I say quietly.

"Yeah, but when you're ninety you can look back and remember what a hottie you gave it up to. All I have to remember is a forty-one-and-a-half-second encounter with Ryan Honeywood in the wet leaves behind his garage. I walked home with mulch in my undies, wondering what all the fuss was about. Good thing Steve Swanson knew what he was doing. After that first romp in the back of his van, I saw the light!"

When I'm ninety will I still be chatting with Michael through my window?

The toaster oven clicks, and I scorch my fingers fishing the bagels out. I slide a plate across the table and wish Rachael hadn't made such a mess with the salt.

"Thanks," she says, and plunks down a huge glob of cream cheese. "I shouldn't be eating dairy, but today I'll make an exception." She looks up from her bagel with this strange look on her face. It's sort of like the look Gabby gets when she's sitting on some incredible gossip. "I, um, brought something for you."

"Oh?" Condoms? Drugs? Vibrator?

"And I want you to keep an open mind."

I hope it's not a vibrator. At least I think I hope it's not. Rachael has actually made owning a vibrator sound sort of appealing.

She bites off a big piece of her bagel and runs off to the entryway. She comes back, unzips her huge crochet purse, and pushes a hair-coloring kit in front of me.

"I'm not dying my hair purple."

She jabs her finger at the model on the box. "Not purple, blond, and it's just highlights!"

"Oh, I'm sorry, *Mom*, I thought I was talking to my friend Rachael, who'd never imply that my hair sucks just because it's 'mousy.'"

Rachael laughs. "Your mom and I don't usually see eye to eye, but I think she's right on this one."

A beautiful woman on the front of the box is smiling and showing off her very white teeth while some unseen fan blows her blond hair back attractively. Whenever the wind blows my hair, it ends up looking like greasy spaghetti.

"Highlights are just not me. I'm happy the way I am."

"They're no big deal. They'll just give you a little lift, a little self-confidence for tonight."

"What, Danny won't like me the way I am?"

"This isn't for Danny, it's for you. And I can do just a few to frame your face, but more will look better. Trust me, you'll love it."

So I sit while Rachael blow-dries my hair. Why did I let her do this? I mean, I stopped reading *Cosmo* and all of those other stupid magazines in eighth grade because of the demoralizing messages they were sending to mousy, broken teens like myself. And yet here I am, sitting in my bathroom feeling light-headed from the dye's noxious fumes.

"Oh no, the Stagano twins are always sporting these nasty roots. Will I have a paved black highway running up the middle of my scalp in a month? I will kill you if I end up looking like the Stagano twins!" I yell.

"Marissa and Mimi bleach their entire heads, and they have black hair to begin with. This is way more subtle," Rachael says, turning off the dryer. "Ta-da!"

I open my eyes.

Wow.

I look different. I turn my head and check out the sides. I think I like it. I like it a lot. I hate that I like it.

"Well? Say something, and you'll be lying if you say it doesn't look great."

"It's . . . okay, but it goes against everything I stand for. I should feel good about myself just because, not because my hair looks . . ." I stare at myself some more.

"Because my hair looks great!" I wish I could stop smiling. "But I feel like I've sold out."

Rachael is laughing. "Look, you're thinking about this way too much. Highlights are not supposed to be some life-altering thing. They're just for fun, for a boost. And if you'd spent the summer at the beach instead of hiding in your room, this is what you'd look like. It's beach in a bottle, that's all."

"My mom is going to love this. I hate that she is going to love this." I pick up the hairbrush and pull it through my hair. "And you will get major bonus points with her for doing it."

Rachael looks in the mirror and rakes her fingers through her hair. "You needed something to get you out of your funk, and playing with my hair always makes me feel better. And I read in one of my books about how teens pierce and color and stuff because it's one thing we have control over, and you know, it's really true. It's powerful."

"Yeah, but this was your idea, not mine. The power is all yours."

Rachael rolls her eyes and shrugs. "Well, you still look good."

The phone rings and I run to my room to get it.

"Hello?"

"Hi, um, Jordan. It's me, Danny."

Yea! I sit at my desk and write his name on a piece of paper.

"Hi, Danny." I wonder if he can tell I'm smiling. I feel like my smile is winging its way through the phone lines. I shake my hair and smile some more.

"Um, I don't know if you've talked to Janine or Gabby or anything, but they mentioned this party, and uh . . ."

I'm sooo happy! I draw a heart around his name.

"Yeah, they said you might be coming. Do you need a ride?"

"Well, um, that's why I'm calling."

Uh-oh. He sounds more nervous than usual. Danger! Danger!

"I, um, called Janine to find out where the party was, because, um, my mom wanted to talk to that Mark guy's parents, and . . ."

Oh, shit!

"Mark's parents aren't going to be there," I say quietly.

"Yeah, that's what Janine's brother told me. She wasn't home when I called, so Noah, um, filled me in. Look, my mom always has to check out the scene before she'll let me go anywhere, and honestly, it doesn't sound like my kind of thing. I'm really sorry, but I'll, um . . . maybe we can do something some other time, okay?"

"Sure, call me." I hang up the phone.

I feel totally flat. The highlights rush is gone. But isn't that the way it is with rushes? I draw a big X through the heart I drew.

"Dahling, was that Gabby?" Rachael asks as she walks in my room and strikes a pose. She is wearing the green snake-print dress and a pair of my mother's shoes.

"Danny's not coming. It's not his kind of scene."

"Oh, crap, I'm sorry." Rachael comes in and sits on my bed. She's trying to look sympathetic, but she's in that stupid dress, and I just want to be alone.

"You know, this is a sign I shouldn't go to this party. I'm, I don't know, not wanting to get all trashed tonight, you know? I don't want to listen to Gabby's spin on why Danny is a no-show. I don't want to get all wasted, and I don't want to end up with some guy's hand down my pants or worse, because I know that's what will happen if I go, you know?"

"You just said 'you know' three times in, like, one sentence. You need to get out and socialize. And you can just go to hang out."

I glare at Rachael, but I know it's not her fault Danny blew me off. Not his kind of thing? This party has been my kind of thing for a while. Does that mean I'm not his kind of thing either? Is it over again already?

"Look, Janine told me you've been missing in action lately." She eyes the bottle of rum. "And if we leave you home you'll just get trashed by yourself. Who knows, maybe you'll meet someone new, someone more like you."

"I thought Danny was my type." And frankly, I'm not interested in meeting someone like me.

"Look, I don't know if he is or isn't. Just come to the party and have a good time."

"I really don't want to get trashed tonight."

"No one is going to *make* you get trashed."

She doesn't get it. I can't go and just have a good time. I will plan on turning down a beer or a joint or the coke right until the damn line is stinging a path up my nose and down the back of my throat. Then I will plan on being good at the next party.

I am never good.

And what about Michael? Does he have some vampire spider-sense-is-tingling thing? Will he be able to follow me two towns over? Will I get a free night out, or am I setting myself up for some sort of ambush? Do I care anymore?

"Fine, I'll go," I say.

What do I have to lose?

CHAPTER NINE

I'm looking at the trees whizzing by outside the car window, and now I know why I've been hiding out in my house these past months. Michael could be absolutely anywhere, and I'm insane to have come out. My heart is pounding faster than the bass blasting from the speakers. Gabby is in the front seat, singing along to an old Nirvana song like she's Annie Warbucks. Giving Kurt Cobain the Kiddie-Broadway treatment usually would've had me roaring, but all I want is to be home, safe in my room.

I look over at Rachael. She's singing along, too, oblivious to the fact that Michael could be flying bat-style above the car, waiting to get us when we step out into the night. Can Michael really turn into a bat? Why have I never asked him if he can turn into a bat?

What the hell was I thinking? That I didn't care if Michael was out there? That I didn't care what happened to me? Funny thing is, sitting here now I realize I care so much I'm afraid my heart will burst.

Deep breaths.

Okay, Michael is expecting me to be a good little girl, waiting at home for him like I've done every night since he reappeared. I've given him no reason to think otherwise. Hell, I came very close to letting him in last night, so he'll definitely be itching to give that window thing another go. As far as I know he has no clue who Mark Menducci is; he has absolutely no way of knowing where I'm going tonight. I'm sleeping over at Rachael's, and while it's possible he would go there looking for me, I don't think he would risk being seen by her.

I think.

But what if Michael somehow knows I've had an epiphany of sorts today? What if he can sense I've finally made up my mind, and even though Danny dumped me I don't want to be with Michael?

I can't believe I have to break up with Michael again.

Oh God, would Michael move down his list of ex-girlfriends and start making his own vampire cheerleading squad?

I'm not even going there.

But if I meet up with Michael, would he attack or let the choice be mine? He says he loves me, and chances are he hasn't had any sort of epiphany today. He still thinks we had something special, and I seriously doubt Michael even knows what an epiphany is.

"Oh, crap! We didn't bring bathing suits," Gabby calls out over the music. "Mark's pool is still open, and he said he'll have the heat cranked up. Of course, that won't bother you, will it Rachael?"

Rachael rolls her eyes. "There's no shame in being comfortable with your body!"

Gabby laughs. "Yeah, you've whipped your tits out so often, the thrill is gone."

I shake my head. Everyone *has* seen Rachael's tits, many, many times, but Gabby doesn't need to make a stink about it. At practically every party since freshman year, Rachael finds some excuse to bare her breasts. I wonder if the guys *do* care anymore. She's hung them out the car windows more times than I can count, titillating teenage boys with her bare-breasted Amazon Princess routine. It's amazing the warrior boobs haven't caused any accidents, really. I fully expect to see her on one of the MTV Spring Break shows where the girls are yanking their tops off, and only a blacked-out rectangle dancing across their chests saves their fathers at home from a trip to the ER. Of course, if some dad is watching that stuff, he gets what he deserves.

But maybe guys never get sick of seeing tits?

"Hey, Rachael, is all of your hair purple?" Gabby yells back, and she and Janine take to fits in the front seat.

"You'll have to wait and see," she replies, laughing.

She leans over to me and whispers, "It's totally waxed—everything!"

"Oh my God!" I'm laughing now, too. It feels good, really good. I want to feel good again. Maybe I *will* meet someone tonight. I'm going to relax and have fun and see what happens. Michael and Danny can go screw each other for all I care! This is the start of a new me. Tonight I start taking control! I sit up straight in my seat and start singing along.

Janine turns down the music. "Damn! Look at all the cars. We're going to have to walk, like, half a mile to get to the house."

"No!" I yell, too loud.

"Easy there," Rachael says, eyebrows raised.

"Couldn't you drop us off at his house and then park?" It's amazing how quickly I can go from self-assured to quivering Jell-O girl.

"I'm not a chauffeur!" Janine snaps.

"But, Jeeves, that's what Mumsy and Daddy pay you for," Gabby says.

"That's not what I meant," I say, kicking the back of Gabby's seat. "I just want to get the party started, you know? It's been so long since I've been out." I slump in my seat as they all start whooping it up and cheering. Couldn't they hear the total lack of enthusiasm in my voice?

"Thatta girl!" Janine says. "Tonight is gonna rock!"

Gabby and Rachael start singing that Pink song about getting the party started as Janine parks the car alongside some bushes. You could fit five houses from my neighborhood in the space between the houses here, and apparently the very rich do not believe in streetlights. The darkness provides perfect cover for vampires stalking their ex-girlfriends.

Of course, my side of the car is inches from some very thick hedges that anyone or anything could be lurking behind. I can't move. I can't make my hand move to open the door. God, I can't even control my hands lately.

Gabby slams her door and opens mine. "*Après vous*, mademoiselle."

Her voice is like a trigger, and I jump out of the car and wrap my arm around hers.

"*Merci.*" I'm guessing it's better to get out than get left behind alone in the car. I wonder if vampires have to be invited into cars, or if it's just a house thing?

I link my other arm with Rachael's. "Brrrr, it's cold!" I say, so they won't know I'm using them as human shields.

My eyes are darting back and forth across the street, checking out the shadows—so far so good. I figure if Michael was going to strike, it would've been right when we got out, when he'd think we weren't expecting anything. That's what I would have done, and I certainly don't expect Michael to come up with anything too complex.

I can hear the music now, and I stop clutching their arms so tightly. We're almost there, and we're rushing through the cold air, arms all linked. I'm starting to smile. Michael isn't anywhere near here. I'm free for the night—

Gabby stops suddenly, pulling us all back.

A small squeak escapes from my throat. Is it Michael?

"We're off to see the Wizard, the wonderful Wizard of Oz," Gabby belts out as she starts us forward again with an added skip to our walk.

I laugh and start singing along, wondering if the Wizard could drop his hands in his sack and bring out something for me—maybe a little self-control.

CHAPTER TEN

I've been to six parties at Mark Menducci's, but I'm still blown away by how the über-rich live. Is it really necessary to have arcade-style video games in one's home? Is it really necessary to have a heated swimming pool with two attached Jacuzzis? I don't know what Mark's father does, but I'd guess he's not around much, and as far as I know there isn't a mother or stepmother—there aren't any personal photos around to document a mom, at least.

I scan the living room as Gabby and Janine head off to talk to Mark; it's mostly theater and band kids from our school. I recognize a bunch of guys, Mark's local friends, from the other parties, but can't remember any of their names. The smell of pot is thick in the air, but I can't see anyone partaking. Rachael points to the patio, where a small crowd is gathered around the kegs. That will do for starters. We start to head out and I'm glad to see someone is tapping a new one. I'm so sick of my mother's liquor cabinet.

"Look who's back from the dead!" someone shrieks.

My heart skips two beats as that scream echoes off the fifty-foot ceilings. I turn around, relieved to find it's just Kassie Campbell flinging her arms around me. The entire room is staring at me, but not in a bad way. I think they're relieved that none of them will have to sit through a Kassie talk marathon. I see two people pointing at me, mouthing the word "sucker."

"Where the *h-e*-double-*l* hell have you been, girl?"

Kassie has obviously been here for a while. She digs her fingers into my shoulders to keep her balance. I turn my head away from her face to ward off another beer breath attack. It's interesting how disgusting beer breath is when you haven't had any yourself.

"Uh, I'll get you a drink," Rachael says, scurrying away.

"Oh, me too! Me too! Get me one," Kassie calls out.

"Hi, Kassie," I say. I try to smile at her. She does seem to be genuinely pleased to see me. I guess we must have classes in opposite wings this year because I think the last time I saw her was at Melissa Smith's track party.

"What did you do to your hair? It looks so tremendo!"

"It was Rachael's idea."

Kassie looks around the room, smirking. "Why doesn't she do this to her hair? I mean what is up with like the purple? Heinous!"

I shrug. "Everyone's got their own thing, I guess."

Kassie nods and snorts with laughter. I really don't think she needs another beer. But then, I guess she's like the rest of us: keep drinking until you puke or your ride wants to go home. Not that I have any intention of binge drinking tonight.

"You *must* sit with me, Jordan," she says, dragging me to an empty space on a leather couch. "I *must* know where you've been. Why didn't you go out for the cross-country team? Coach has been, like, this total Nazi—majorly riding our asses. We need you. And I told *everyone* that you were gonna be part of the set crew. I mean, like, after you did such a tremendo job on *Brigadoon*, I just figured Jordan Malone would be out there, you know, leading the paint crew. It's not too late, you know—you can still help. And they *need* help! The fucking sets are, like, all mud-colored, it looks like a monkey painted them. And who the hell ever heard of *Dark of the Moon*, anyway? The show's a tremendo bummer; I'm sooo glad I didn't get a part. And someone put dog shit in the witches mud." She starts laughing and digs her fingers into my arm again.

I wrinkle my nose. I think that's an appropriate response for the barrage I've just sat through.

"The witches put the mud on their fucking faces!" she screams.

She's rocking back and forth laughing her head off.

"Excuse me, Jordan, I have a delivery."

I look up and a guy with deep green eyes is handing me a beer. He looks familiar, and my stomach does a nervous flip, like I've just realized I've forgotten something important.

"Rachael said you are in desperate need of liquid salvation."

I nod and take it. "Thanks."

"Hey, where's mine? She was supposed to get me one, too." Kassie pouts.

"Sorry, she didn't mention anyone else," he says, sitting down on my other side.

He has a nice voice. Smooth.

"Well, we'll just see about that! Rachael thinks she's all *that* with her stupid purple hair, but she's not, let me tell you! She's—"

"Whoa, Kassie, this may or may not have been an obvious slam, but I think you need to talk to Rachael and clear the air," I suggest.

Kassie apparently thinks this is a tremendo idea, and springs off the couch, nearly upending me. I narrowly avoid soaking Mr. Green Eyes' pants with beer, but the carpet takes the hit. I'll assume Mark will get the entire house professionally cleaned tomorrow so I don't bother with it. Kassie stumbles off to the patio and my rescue hero points up to the balcony above us.

Rachael wiggles her eyebrows at me and points to my new friend. She mouths the word "cute." I think she sent this guy over to be helpful, maybe to lift my spirits, but I can't help but feel I've just been pimped out. My cheeks are burning, but when I turn back, my new buddy is watching Kassie try to get the screen door back into its track—missing, I hope, my exchange with Rachael.

"Thanks, you saved me," I say.

He smiles at me. Nice smile. Really nice green eyes.

"You don't remember my name, do you?" His smile turns sly.

Oh, great, did I get all gropey with this guy and completely forget? I will kill Rachael if she sent an old flyby guy after me.

"I'm sorry." I'm getting the feeling I've had a close encounter with him, and I'm pretty embarrassed because it's obvious he remembers and I don't. Considering the state in which I left Mark's last party, this really isn't a big shocker. I down what's left of my beer and will my brain cells to regenerate.

He laughs and one cute dimple turns up on his cheek. "Well, I don't think I could forget you. I mean, how many girls confess they've had cockroaches for pets?"

"Bug-boy!"

"I prefer Kyle, actually."

I remember!

It *was* at the last party I went to. I was in the kitchen when I heard some of Mark's friends calling Kyle "Bug-boy." He told them to fuck off, but I went up to him all trashed and asked what was up with the nickname.

He told me about his dad being an entomologist and I got excited. I think I made an absolute fool of myself jabbering about roaches. I hope I wasn't as bad as Kassie.

He leans his arm over the back of the couch, resting it lightly on my shoulders. I take it he's been here awhile, too, to make a move like that so soon. Maybe he just doesn't feel like wasting time with small talk.

"I told my dad I'd met someone who actually had cockroaches for pets; he thinks I should marry you."

"Ha, that's funny." He's staring at me . . . what the hell happened that night? Part of me wonders if we actually made some sort of connection, a connection that beer has erased from my memory.

Kyle leans in and whispers in my ear. "I had to tell him that someone stole you out from under my nose, and you haven't been to the last few parties. I thought you were the one that got away."

The ear thing triggers my memory. What is it about hot breath on ears, anyway? I remember Kyle and I talked forever that night, in a bar-slash-playroom somewhere in the house. He has a perfect sister that his parents worship. His dog's name is Marley, after the ghost. The only question left is how did I end up with Matt Walberg in the pool house? Kyle is way cuter than Matt. What was I thinking? And how did Matt intercept my love connection with Bug-boy?

I look over and he's smiling. He knows he's getting to me, but, well, I have absolutely no idea what to say next. I suppose his dad and I could talk about roach food, but I don't know a thing about Kyle. Besides Marley and his sister, that is.

I need more beer.

"Um, I think I'll get another beer. Do you want one, too?" That's good, a polite offer. We can talk about beer.

"Or we can go to the barroom in the basement and pick up where we left off. Bonus is we can drink from bottles, you know, so we won't have to fight the keg foam. Come on."

Do I want to go? I'm not sure. Kyle's hot, and maybe Rachael's right. Maybe it would be nice to meet—well, in this case, reacquaint myself with—someone new, but I have to admit a part of me is still thinking about Danny. I don't look at Kyle and get all quivery. Okay, I get a *little* quivery when his mouth is on my ear, and I did tell him about the hissers, but if I'm serious about this "new me" crap, I will stay upstairs, drink just one or two more beers, and play catch-up with Gabby, Rachael, and Janine.

I scan the room, then the pool area—looks like Rachael is already half naked in the hot tub. She's so tall, her boobs bob on top of the water. The other girls don't look so pleased to see the warrior breasts all wet and perky, but it looks like quite a few guys are stripping down to their underwear to get closer to them. And there's Gabby in a corner with Kassie; she's yelling and laughing about some "asshole." At least she looks like she's enjoying herself.

Kyle stands up and holds out his hand. "It's okay,

I've got Mark's permission to bring fellow bug lovers down there."

Why couldn't Rachael have rescued me from Kassie? Why did she have to send Kyle?

Say no. Say no.

"Okay, we can go down and just *talk*." I'm hoping he heard my emphasis on the word talk.

"Sure thing."

He takes my hand and starts walking. He's not letting go of my hand, and I'm thinking maybe he didn't quite get my gist.

I'm still in control, though, and this will be good practice.

We'll just talk.

Just talk.

CHAPTER ELEVEN

His mouth is hot and wet, kissing my neck, heading down. I realize I've been on autopilot. My mouth and hands are doing what they're supposed to be doing, given the situation, but it's like it's not really happening. I don't feel anything. The noises I'm making are just for show, not the result of any real burst of passion. I wish I could get back in the zone, because it's too hard to keep up the show now that I'm conscious of doing it. He heads back up to my mouth and nibbles on my lower lip, then over to my ear. He slides his fingers under my waistband and across my stomach.

I'm definitely not feeling the tingle now. I'm feeling nothing, and I want to stop. No, I *need* to stop this now while I still can.

He's panting hard on my neck, rubbing himself on my leg, and fumbling with the button of my jeans.

"Wait," I say, pushing his hands away.

He leans in, kissing my neck, nibbling on my ear. All of a sudden it feels so practiced—like he got his hands on an issue of his sister's *Cosmo* and read about the ear thing causing spontaneous orgasms.

His hand makes its way down to the button on my jeans again. "It's okay."

I'm not going to do this. I push his hands away again. "I said stop!"

He's staring at me as if I'm crazy; the whites of his eyes seem to glow in the dark room. I grab my shirt and pull it back on, static crackles through my hair. For a split second I worry about how my hair looks and actually turn away from him and smooth it down.

Oh, God. There are at least three other couples down here in various states of arousal. How had I not noticed them? Where the hell is my bra?

"What's the problem?" he asks.

I hug my arms around my chest. "I just don't want to do this. I didn't want to let things go this far."

He regains his composure and smiles, putting his hand on my shoulder. He leans in and whispers, "We can go slow. I can go real slow."

I push him back, feeling the heat radiating off his bare chest. "I don't even know you."

He stands up and adjusts his pants. His eyes don't

look so nice now. Is this why I never say no—to avoid this look of contempt?

"That hasn't stopped you before."

Now it's my turn to ice over. "What does that mean?"

I immediately wish I hadn't asked, because I know exactly what he's talking about—and I know he isn't going to be nice when he throws my words back in my face.

Kyle picks up his beer and takes a long swig. "It means you've hooked up with some guy at every one of these parties, and everyone knows you're a sure thing who doesn't mind that a morning-after phone call will not be forthcoming. If I'd known you were trying to reclaim your virginity, I wouldn't have listened to your friend when she suggested you needed some fun." He adjusts the front of his pants again.

Then he reaches down and picks up my bra, tossing it onto my lap. There are tread marks on the cups from his sneakers.

"Well, I guess I'll go see what's left from the pickings Mark ordered from your school. It may be too late for the good ones, but in the dark, you all look the same." He finishes off his beer and slams it down roughly on the end table. "And, for your edification, bugs make my skin crawl."

He turns and heads up the basement stairs, leaving me sitting in the room filled with moans and wet noises. I cram my bra in my pocket and pull down my shirt to cover the straps that stick out.

"*You* make my skin crawl," I whisper, though I know the ugly, squirmy feeling coursing down my spine is all my own doing.

So I sit, the only one not coupled or coupling in the basement. I want to get out of here, but my legs won't move.

I think I'm just afraid to go upstairs. I wonder what wonderful things Kyle is saying about me—if I'll get the evil eye from all of Mark's friends?

I wonder if they're talking about the "pickings" behaving badly tonight?

What are the chances Janine is ready to go home?

I look out the large picture windows put in to brighten this basement lair, and I see a clump of girls talking at the edge of Mark's property. They're in a semi-circle, with their backs to me, but I can tell they're excited. There's a lot of hair flipping and head bobbing. It looks like they're laughing.

They don't look familiar. One girl is wearing a Sands Point jacket. They must be Mark's friends. Maybe some girls from Mark's school are enjoying the pickings from North Shore. One girl turns and heads back to the house and I see him.

Michael.

My heart skips a beat. I gasp and gulp for air. Michael is here. He's talking to people. He's followed me. I can see his eyes darting past the group toward the house. Is he looking for me? I can't believe he really came. I can't believe he'd take the risk of coming around where people could recognize him.

I crouch down, afraid he'll see me. Can he sense I've spotted him?

Bug-boy is suddenly looking really good.

Michael gives one of the girls a hug. While his head is over her shoulder, nuzzling in, I see him checking out the house.

His eyes are glowing green, like a cat's.

I wonder if that girl likes the coconut stink. Can she smell that other, earthy smell?

I want to turn away; I'm afraid he'll sense me looking at him, but I've wanted to see his face for three months. In the soft light that bathes Mark's yard I see that he still looks like Michael; the green animal glow is the only giveaway. Part of me is relieved, but maybe looking human makes him more dangerous.

He's hugging that girl; I can feel his arms around her, squeezing her hard, too hard. She breaks away and takes a step back. Did she sense something wrong with Michael? Is it obvious what he is if you're that close to him?

I've got to get out of here. I need to make my move now. But will I have time to get to a car before he knows what I'm doing?

I race up the stairs and pause at the top step. The living room is mostly empty, except for Kassie sobbing on the couch. Nobody's paying any attention to her. Where is Janine? Where is anyone I know? Has most of the North Shore crew left already? Will one of Mark's friends invite Michael in?

I look out to the pool; it seems most of the party has migrated out there. Topless girls are jumping off the diving board to claps and cheers from the guys in the pool. Steam is rising off the water, fogging my view of the backyard. Michael won't risk getting too close to the house. There are too many people who would recognize him.

Where the *hell* is Janine?

I start toward the kitchen, but Kyle is in there with a couple of guys who are pounding on his shoulder as if to say, "Sorry you didn't get laid, Bug-boy."

I look back at Kassie lying on the couch, crying into a pillow. Did she drive here? Of course, she doesn't look like she's remotely able to operate a car right now.

How many beers have I had? I look at my watch. I've been here over four hours, I had maybe five beers or six, most of them pounded within the first two hours before the make-out session began. According to beer-math, I am probably over the legal limit, but I should be able to drive without taking out anyone's hedge.

I am certainly feeling extremely alert. God bless adrenaline.

I hunch over and scurry to Kassie. "Hey, what's wrong?" It's taking "tremendo" effort to keep my voice calm.

Kassie looks up. She's got snot pouring out of her nose and white powder smeared across her cheek. I know how bad it feels to be drunk and coked up at the same time—the two different highs fighting in your body. I'm glad I didn't know they were cutting lines up here; my heart is beating fast enough as it is.

"This party sucks!" she says, and rests her head back on the pillows, letting out a huge moan. "I feel sick."

I start rubbing her back, trying not to grimace as she lets loose a vomit-smelling burp. I turn my head away and take a deep breath. "Why don't you let me take you home? You brought your car, right?"

She's not saying anything. Does she even hear me?

"Kassie, do you want to go home?" I say a little louder.

She looks up and wipes her nose on her sleeve. She's nodding yes, sniffling.

"Do you have your keys? Where's your car?" I hope it's not too far away from the front door. I hope it's not blocked in.

Kassie sucks in a gallon of snot and looks around the room. "My purse. Red."

I look around the room, searching for her purse, or someone else I can get a ride from.

Where *is* Janine?

"There," Kassie whispers, pointing to the marble breakfast bar. "Red. Armani."

She flops back onto the couch, and I run over and grab her purse. I dump it on the counter. Hairbrush, wallet, diet pills, *keys*! Mercedes. I wonder if her parents know she gets trashed and drives their ridiculously expensive car around? I sweep everything but the diet pills back in. She can't weigh more than ninety pounds.

"Let's go," I say into her ear. She's not moving, and I'm tempted to just take her car. I'd be doing her a favor, but I don't want to add grand theft auto to my list of troubles. "Come on," I grunt, pulling one of her arms up.

"Leave me alone," she says, swiping her hand at me.

"Oh, no, you're going home!" I yank her up on her feet and she opens her eyes, surprised.

"Jordan! I haven't like seen you in . . ." She's staring at me, and I think she's starting to remember our conversation from before.

"I'm taking you home," I say, leading her toward the door.

"Oh, yeah," she mumbles. "I don't feel so good."

"You can puke later. Let's just get you and me out of here."

"Coat, I need my coat."

Damn! I forgot about our coats. Where are they? Screw it!

"Look, let's just get out of here and get our coats tomorrow, okay."

"Mmm. I'm staying at my dad's this weekend."

"Okay, then. Great."

I'm holding Kassie up and peeking out the window by the door. Judging by the amount of cars in the driveway, the party has cleared out considerably. I look at all the cars for a Mercedes. "What color is it?"

"I feel sick," she moans again.

"Your car, what color is it?"

She's not saying anything. I'm trying to stay patient, but coddling her is getting real old, real fast. "Kassie, what color is your *freaking* car?"

Her head lolls on its side. "Silver," she whispers.

Down at the end of the driveway is a silver car. I think it's a Mercedes. How fast can I get to the car dragging Kassie? I can't do it quickly enough. It's too risky. I turn around and a guy pops up from the basement barroom.

"Hey, can you help me?"

He looks over and smiles. His face is all flushed and I wonder what the girl he was just with is doing now. Basking in the afterglow? Passed out? Did he see Bugboy and me going at it?

He smirks. "Hey, baby, the Bradster can help you any way you want any time you want."

The Bradster? Oh, please.

"I just need help getting her to the car." I tilt my head toward Kassie and hope he gets it.

He looks disappointed, but he's coming over. "Whoa, looks like too much party, party, party."

"Yeah, way too much." I open the door and peer out. No Michael. No Michael that I can see, at any rate.

"Yo, Steve-man," the Bradster calls out. "Little help here."

Steve-man starts coming toward us, and from the slant he's walking on, it's apparent he's almost as gone as Kassie.

"Dude," Steve-man says, nodding. His face is red and sweaty.

"Help me haul this chick, man."

"Cool," Steve-man says, still nodding, looking Kassie up and down. He wiggles his eyebrows at the Bradster. "Hottie."

I'm very tempted to just throw Kassie at their feet and take her car, but I decide to try again, this time a little more direct. "Yo, Steve-man, this hottie may very well start puking all over the place if we don't get her out of here fast!"

"Dude, that would suck," the Bradster says, looking around, and I bet he's wishing he was still down in the basement. But Steve-man and the Bradster seem to think the threat of projectile vomiting is a good reason for removing Kassie from the premises, and they each grab an end of her.

"Mark, like, owes us one," Steve-man grunts as he wobbles with his arms around Kassie's chest. "Cause, like, puking sucks."

"Silver Mercedes at the end," I say. I let them go out first. I do a side-to-side rapid scan of the bushes. Kassie moans and slaps her hands around Steve-man's face.

"Cut the shit," he says, stumbling toward the car.

I take a deep breath and sprint to the car. I shove the keys in and open the door. "Hurry up!" I yell, watching the Bradster laugh as Kassie relentlessly flails at Steve-man. I fire up the engine and tap the steering wheel, counting their steps. God, why are they so slow? I look around the hedges. I can't see into the backyard. Where is Michael?

Steve-man and the Bradster come around, and I lean over to unlock the passenger door. They dump her in and shake their heads. "She's, like, totally whacked," the Bradster says.

"Everyone here is totally whacked," I say.

Steve-man closes his eyes, nodding. "Yo, that is so true. You're so . . ."

I lean over Kassie and slam her door.

"Later!" I hit the door lock and throw the car into reverse, squealing backward down the driveway and nearly hitting several cars parked behind us. "Put on your seatbelt, Kassie." I look toward the house and I think I see Michael standing on a small hill in the side yard. I'm pretty sure it's him, but I'm not stopping for a closer look. I'm getting out of here. I hope the Bradster and the other guests will be okay. Maybe I should have warned someone.

Kassie groans and looks my way. "You're sho nice."

"Yeah, thanks."

She nods. "I don't think you're a slut."

"Great, glad to hear it."

We head onto Route One and I try to decide where to go. "Look, Kassie, maybe we should drive around a bit. I mean, I don't think you want your dad seeing you like this, right?"

Kassie shuts her eyes and her breaths get deeper. I wonder what makes a person a slut. Am I a slut because I let a bunch of guys in without the required relationship? Is Rachael a slut because she likes having sex?

"You're sho nice," Kassie murmers.

Am I a slut because I let Michael in so fast? I guess the third date is pretty fast considering I'd only let David Santos get to an over-the-bra second base before that.

But, hell, things have gotten a lot faster since. Does it count if you don't always enjoy it? I wish Kassie was awake; I'd ask her. I wonder if Kassie's done it.

I turn onto Shore Road. The back roads may have fewer cops on them, but Shore Road has fewer places for Michael to hide. The car's got plenty of gas, and Kassie seems to be somewhat comatose. I'll just drive around until sunrise, or pull into the beach parking lot and hang out. I can rehearse what I'm going to say to Michael. And I can figure out what I'm going to tell Kassie's father when I drop her off.

"Sorry, Mr. Campbell, I'd have brought Kassie home earlier but I couldn't risk getting out of the car until the sun rose. You see, I blew off my vampire ex-boyfriend and you know how unpredictable the undead can be. I mean, really, Mr. Campbell, would you ever have imagined he'd come looking for me? Would you ever have imagined he'd show up at the party and actually talk to people? He's getting bolder, that's for sure."

Mr. Campbell will nod knowingly. *"Or desperate. Do you think he'd have risked exposure if he'd been thinking rationally?"*

"You have a point, sir, but I assessed the situation and got myself out before there was any trouble. And I didn't sleep with anyone."

Mr. Campbell will smile proudly and say, *"You learned a good lesson, young lady. Never trust a vampire—or men in general, ha, ha. Well, good luck, and thanks for taking such good care of my little girl."*

I'll look up and smile at him. *"And she didn't puke in your car."*

I decide to pull into the Bayville Beach parking lot and turn off the engine. It's open in all directions so there's no way Michael can sneak up on me. The sky is getting lighter and the coast is clear—no pun intended. I imagine Michael must be getting his affairs in order so he can sleep. I wonder where he sleeps? There's so much I've never asked him, so many times we just glossed over the fact that he's dead.

But maybe he thought my not knowing the ins and outs of being a vampire would make it easier for me to open the window. Maybe that's why he climbs the tree instead of flying into it bat-style: so I wouldn't see how low I'd have to sink to be with him.

What do I do now? I know I'm stronger than I thought—well, at least I know I'm capable of saying no, and that's a start. And I don't want anything Michael has to offer. It's probably too late for Danny and me, but we won't even get a chance if I stay in my room hiding from Michael. How the hell am I going to get rid of Michael?

I need to think about something else. I put my bra back on, then take out my phone.

I should check my messages to see if Janine or Rachael were trying to figure out where I ended up. I open my purse and turn on my cell phone.

Jesus, twelve messages.

"Shut up, you assholes. I can't hear myself talk. Jordie-pie, Gabby here,"

"And Janine! Give me the damn phone! Anyway, Mark has some awesome weed. Where are you hiding?

Get off whatever guy you're on, figuratively and literally, and get out to the pool house. P.S., it's like twelve-fifty, so if you don't get this soon, fugetaboutit!"

Sorry, Gab, I was sucking face with Bug-boy.

"Oh, God, Jordan, it's Lisa. Don't come home, he's waiting for you. He's alive, and, oh, God, call home. It's Lisa and I'm at your house. Please call me. Michael is alive and . . . I think he's gone after you. Call me as soon as you get this."

Lisa? Lisa's at my house? She's seen Michael? Shit! Oh, Shit! How did Lisa get in my house? How did she get my cell phone number?

"Hey, Jordan, it's Janine. Where are you? I'm, like, ready to go and there's no sign of you. That guy Kyle is, like, with someone else, so where are you? Find someone better? Hope you're having fun!!!"

"Jordan, where are you? I'm scared. I'm so scared. I think I'm going crazy. What if he comes back? I don't know what I'll do if he comes back. Your mom and Steve aren't home, and Jordan—please call me."

"Jordan, be careful."

"Jordan, where are you? Jordan . . ."

I turn off the phone and I look at my watch. Forty-five minutes until sunrise—Kassie should be sober enough to take the wheel. I gently shake her shoulder. "Hey, wake up."

Kassie's head jerks forward, and she opens her eyes. "What?" She looks out the windshield and yawns. "Where are we?"

"At the beach, but I need you to drive me home."

CHAPTER TWELVE

I watch Kassie's car pull away and hustle to my front door. Could Lisa still be here? How did she get in, anyway? Why did she come to see me?

Nutty meows and winds his way through my legs as I open the door.

He zips into the kitchen, and I stand in the front entrance and listen—nothing but the sound of kibble being consumed. Is she still here?

I head up the stairs, thankful for the God-awful pink carpeting my mom put in that's making my ascent quiet. I don't know why, but I'm a little scared to see Lisa. Well, not as scared as I was to see Michael last night, but Lisa was my best friend for nine years, and I don't know what I'm going to say to her.

I open my bedroom door, careful to pull down on the knob to avoid it squeaking. Lisa is curled up against the wall opposite the window. She didn't even bother to get a pillow or blankets. Maybe she was too scared to go back toward the window.

Why didn't I ever think to move my bed to the other wall?

Lisa looks frail, so unlike how I remember her. She was always strong, kind of like Rachael, but not so in-your-face, and even though she was one of the shortest girls in our class, when you talked to her she seemed tall. And Lisa was brave. When we climbed my tree she always jumped down six feet to the ground, her red curls flying past me as I hung on to the lowest branch, prolonging the drop as long as possible.

"Lisa?"

Lisa's eyes open, and she's staring at me like she's not sure if I'm really there. "Jordan?"

"Yeah, hi. I'm, um, home." Lisa isn't moving; she's just staring. I want to tell her to blink. I want to tell her there's nothing to worry about—but that wouldn't exactly be true.

"Jordan, am I crazy? Was that really Michael? He seemed so real, but he couldn't be, could he?"

I walk over and sit down next to her. She pulls herself up slowly and leans into me. I can feel her shaking.

"You're not crazy. I'm so sorry you had to see him. It figures, the one night I go out. . . . But it was Michael—it is Michael. He's . . ."

How much do I tell her? I'd kind of like to leave out the embarrassing I've-been-holed-up-in-my-room-for-three-months-talking-to-a-dead-guy-and-contemplating-joining-him stuff.

"Is he really a vampire?" she asks.

My eyes widen. "He told you?"

She turns away. "It's really true?"

I nod. The lack of sleep is making me punchy. "I'm afraid our former homecoming king is now king of the undead." I try to laugh a little, to throw some levity into this, but Lisa's face crumples.

"I was so scared," she sobs. "I came to see you, and I was waiting for you, and then he shows up at the window."

I walk over to my bed and sit. "He's been coming here every night since his funeral." I turn and secure the latch on the window, then run my fingers down the pane. "Yesterday was the first night I've been out since then."

"He thought I was you. He just started talking, and he sounded so concerned, like . . . like you were still his girlfriend."

"Yeah, well, we're real close."

Lisa's mouth drops open.

"Uh, that's a joke," I say. "Sort of. But I think I'm the only one he's been talking to—until last night, that is. Somehow he followed me to this party. I don't know how he knew where I was, but somehow he did."

"I was praying he wouldn't be able to find you."

"What do you mean?"

She's turned away again, looking at my bookshelf. My eyes gravitate toward the gold-flecked frame of the picture of us that I've turned sideways and tucked away between the books. I wonder if she sees it.

"I kind of looked in your diary and read about the party. I kind of told him." Lisa looks at me, her chin quivering. "But when he realized who he was talking to, and that you weren't home, he went crazy. He said he was going to come in. He said he'd hurt me."

"He can't come in unless you invite him! Didn't you read *that* in my journal?"

"I wasn't exactly thinking clearly! I . . . I just wanted him to go. I didn't think he'd find you. I wasn't even sure if you were really at the party; you wrote that you weren't going, and that entry was from a couple of days ago."

I shake my head. "You read my journal and you sent him after me."

"I'm sorry!"

"We're not fourth grade best-friends-forever who swap diaries anymore!"

"I just . . ."

"What—invaded my privacy, almost got me killed?"

Lisa squeezes her eyes shut and rocks back and forth. "I'm sorry."

"Look, I'm sorry, too. I was pretty messed up the first time Michael showed up, and I won't be getting any awards for good judgment, either. Forget the stupid diary, what're you doing here? How did you even get in? How did you get my cell number?"

Lisa wipes her nose against her sleeve and takes a shaky breath. It's surreal to see her barely holding herself together.

"The number is on your bulletin board." She points at the board and I shake my head. I can never remember my own number, so I put it up where I'd have to see it a lot.

"And I still have your key from when I used to feed Nutty if you were away, or in case of an emergency."

I'm not sure sneaking into my house and reading my diary qualifies as an emergency, but her eyes are wide and hopeful, like I should be totally stoked about this trip down memory lane. I'm guessing now is not the best time to tell her I tossed out her key a few years ago.

"And I wanted to see how you were."

"Well, now you know. Total head case being stalked by a vampire—classic teen angst. How have the last few years been for you?"

Lisa manages the tiniest of smiles. "Pretty sucky, actually."

"Come on . . . tennis all-star, in-crowd, great hair—high school dreams come true."

"I know you know about me being *away*."

I shrug. "Rehab is very Hollywood right now. All the A-listers are doing it."

Lisa sighs and pushes herself up slowly. She walks over to my bed and sits up by my pillow, drawing her knees to her chest. She leans back against the headboard and closes her eyes. "I wasn't in rehab. . . . I was at the Twin Oaks Psychiatric Hospital."

"What? But everyone said . . ."

Lisa opens her eyes and rests her chin on her knees. "You can thank Marnie for the rehab rumor. Apparently, she saw OxyContin in my purse one day and assumed I'd scored it on the street instead of picking it up at Walgreens. After I left for the hospital, she took it upon herself to turn one bottle of pills into a full-blown drug habit—the rest is history."

"But how did you *end up* at the hospital? And what the hell were you doing with OxyContin?"

"After I took a few too many of said pills, my doctor thought I needed a little more supervision—end of story. And right now I'd kind of like to figure out how we're going to deal with Michael instead of discussing my accidental overdose."

I shake my head. "Whoa, wait a minute. You can't drop a bomb like that and expect me to forget about it."

Lisa gets up and walks to my mirror. "I shouldn't have told you. Besides, it was nothing—it was an *accident*."

"An overdose isn't nothing—accidental or not. And you still haven't told me what you were doing with OxyContin in the first place? That's, like, heavy-duty stuff."

"It doesn't matter."

"It does! Lisa, what's going on?"

She looks at me and bites her lower lip.

"You can tell me."

"Fine! I have lupus. And before you ask, it's a *chronic inflammatory disease*—complete with chronic pain, arthritis, headaches, heart and lung problems, and hair loss. Fun, huh?" Lisa runs her fingers through her curls and comes away with a handful of hair. "Oh, and exposure to sunlight brings on this lovely rash. Not real conducive for being out on the courts or attracting guys—not that I have any energy for that."

I look at the red blotches I'd noticed a few days ago splashed across her cheeks. "But isn't there medicine you can take?"

"Yeah, it's just the medicine isn't working that well, but my doctor thinks I'm making *great* strides managing the pain. Only thing left to do is figure out how to live a completely different life from the one I'd imagined. Once I nail that down, I'm hoping to get off the antidepressants."

"Why didn't you tell anyone? What about Alicia? She could've shut Marnie up."

"Alicia? We're real close when I'm playing well, but let's just say most of my friendships revolve around being good at sports. And you know as well as I that if I told everyone I have lupus, there'd be a big pity party with tons of sympathy, and then everyone would slowly back away, leaving me with nothing but my rash."

"No!"

"Yes."

"I don't believe that, but *I'm* here for you, and you've got your parents. Do they even know where you are?"

Lisa sighs. "No. I snuck out after bed check. I couldn't sleep and I needed to clear my head. I wasn't planning to stay out all night, but then Michael showed up."

"Well, when your parents wake up and find you missing, they're gonna freak."

Lisa nods. "I know. I'll call them soon." She stretches her arms over her head as she walks over to my desk chair. "The important thing right now is: What are we going to do about Michael?"

Lisa's hand flutters to her cheek and she traces the rash with her fingers so exactly I imagine she's spent a lot of time looking in the mirror. "Is he still *Michael*? I mean, is he still the way he was before?"

"I think so. He sounds the same. He doesn't have a soul, but he still . . ." I pause because I was about to say he still loves me, but now I'm wondering if that's possible. Can you love someone if you don't have a soul?

Lisa is staring at me intently, waiting for me to finish.

"But, well, you wouldn't know it," I say finally. "He can still be kind of a jerk, but that's nothing new. And he still has feelings," I add, thinking maybe you *can* still feel love without a soul.

"Is that why you haven't done anything about him?"

"Yeah, and . . ." I want to tell Lisa the truth, but I can't. "I suppose I was hoping one of these nights he'd just stop showing up." I push my lips into a smile and keep my focus on Lisa's eyes. I resist the urge to look away and brush my bangs aside—which, according to

Rachael, is a body language red alert for lying.

Lisa shakes her head, "You know, Jordan, you haven't changed. You always expect your little problems to go away by themselves. Well, believe me, you've got to deal with things head on."

"Little problems?" I ask, wondering how Lisa thinks my problem with Michael is so trivial. "Are we talking about the same thing? Michael may still be *Michael*, but I've been trapped in my house for the last four months by this 'little problem' capable of draining all the blood from my body!"

"I didn't mean it like that, it's just . . ." Lisa slumps in the chair. "Okay, bottom line is he has to go, right? He went after you last night, and now I know about him—things have changed."

I let out a big sigh. "It's not that simple. I've read a lot about vampires, and getting rid of them isn't easy. And . . ." Here's my chance to tell her that Michael is in love with me, and that until very recently, I thought I might still love him, too.

I flop back onto my bed and close my eyes. "I just don't think it's doable."

I hear Lisa get up and walk over to my bookcase. She starts drumming her fingers across the spines of the books. I open my eyes just in time to see her pull our picture out from in between the books, and then quickly slide it back. "Everything is doable, and if at first you don't succeed, you find another way."

"Yeah, except in this case, not succeeding gets you killed—or worse!"

"Not if we're prepared. I mean, really, how would you do it?"

"I don't know."

"Well, let's make a list. We'll write down all our options, and decide on the best course of action."

Okay, I know Lisa has always been a total list maniac, but doesn't she realize that no matter how much we prepare, chances are still pretty darn good we'd be dead meat by morning? And doesn't she remember how many times she failed to change the world—or me—with her lists? I want to tell her to stop. I want to tell her I won't be slipping back into my old role as her unwavering follower.

Lisa flips over a piece of paper on my desk and picks up a pen. I wish Rachael were here. I have a feeling she wouldn't approach this problem like we were making campaign slogans for a student council election. Of course, Rachael would probably get hung up trying to analyze Michael's motivations, but right now that sounds a hundred times better than one of Lisa's lists.

"Okay," she says. "I know there's a stake through the heart, crosses, and garlic. That's three. Oh, and sunlight, right? What else?"

"You'd need a shitload of garlic to do any damage, but vampires can't swim, so you could drown them, and there's always my personal favorite: decapitation," I say, hoping she'll see the futility in all this. "But I really don't—"

Lisa looks at me, her eyes wide. "Could you really do that? Could you really cut someone's head off?"

"Not someone's, Michael's. But, no! I'm not saying I could or I would. Don't you see how ridiculous this is?"

"So, you're just going to let him hang out here every night?"

"I don't want to, but I'm not sure what else I can do."

"Does he always come at the same time?"

"No, but after I went out last night I have a feeling he'll be here early tonight to talk."

"Do you know where he sleeps?"

"No, we kind of don't talk a lot about him being dead, but what difference does it make? I mean, you can't seriously think going after him is a good idea?"

"I was, you know, just thinking maybe we could do something during the day. That's all I meant."

"Look, I'll talk to him and see if we can work out some sort of deal, because I don't think driving a stake through Michael's heart will be anything like driving a tennis ball down the court. This is Michael Green we're talking about—Michael Green with supernatural strength to go with his superego."

Lisa stares down at the list on the desk. "What if it was me? Could you kill me?"

"No! God, what are you talking about?"

"We can't hide from him forever, Jordan. And if we go after him, he might make one of us a vampire, right?" She's running her fingers over her rash again. "If somehow he made me into a vampire," she says, speaking very slowly, "would you go after me? Could you kill me?"

I stare at her in horror. "Lisa, I'm not going to talk

about this. Just let me deal with Michael. Let me see what he says."

"But what if he . . ."

The phone rings. "I'll get it," I say, glad to stop this discussion for a few minutes. I look at the number on the screen. "It's your house!"

Lisa takes a deep breath and hugs her arms around her chest. "You answer it."

"Hello?"

"Jordan? This is Mrs. Dolan, I'm so sorry to be calling at this hour, but I've called everyone else, and . . . well, you haven't by any chance heard from Lisa, have you?"

Her mom's voice sounds so brittle, like she's going to break into pieces from worry.

"She's here—she's okay."

Mrs. Dolan lets out a choked sob, and I walk over to Lisa and hand her the phone.

"Yes, Mother? I spent the night. I just needed to get out. I can walk home. We're kind of busy right now. I'm *fine*; we're just working on a school project. Yes, at seven o'clock in the morning! It's just around the corner—I can walk. Whatever!"

Lisa clicks the phone off and puts it back in the cradle. "She's coming to get me." She heads back to my desk and picks up a pen. "How else could you do it?"

"Look, we've got plenty of time to deal with Michael. Just stay inside after sunset until we can get together again to figure something out."

"I can't wait," she says flatly. She throws the pen down on the desk. "But I guess I don't have a choice because my *fucking* mother's coming to pick me up because she can't leave me out of her sight for five seconds!"

My eyes widen. I don't think I've ever heard Lisa swear. Gabby does it all the time and I don't think twice about it, but hearing Lisa do it is awful. My stomach turns, and I don't know why, but I'm embarrassed for her. "She's just worried. I mean, she didn't know where you were."

Lisa glares at me, and I feel like I'm walking past the upper-crust tables in the cafeteria. I thought if Lisa and I ever reconnected, she'd be the same; everything would be the same. But I did a pretty bang-up job imagining this wonderful relationship with Michael, so what do I know?

"At least she cares," I add.

Lisa smiles. It's not her old I'm-on-top-of-the-world smile, but it isn't a condescending one, either.

"I'm sorry. I'm mad at my mom, not you. But I am worried about you. I don't think you should go after him alone."

"For the hundredth time I never said I was going after Michael tonight! I never said I was going after him at all."

The corners of Lisa's mouth curl up. "So you'll wait until we can handle this together?"

"Yes!"

A horn beeps out front. "That's got to be your mom."

Lisa looks me in the eye. "Don't do anything stupid. Stay put tonight!"

"I will."

Lisa narrows her eyes, and nods her head approvingly. "Good."

The horn blares again.

Lisa looks in the mirror and runs her fingers through her curls. I watch as dozens of strands of hair float down to my rug. "I'll call you—unless my mom takes away my phone."

She walks down the hall, and I hear her feet shuffling down the steps. She used to fly down my stairs—skipping every other step and then jumping past the last three, landing with a thud. But not today. Probably not ever again. I wonder what it feels like to have your body turn on you?

The door slams and I drop down on my bed. I'm glad I'm alone. I need to figure out what I'm going to do—without help from Lisa. I thought it'd be great having someone else help me with Michael, but this doesn't feel right. And with everything Lisa's going through, I don't think she's in the right place to help me with this.

I get up and walk over to my desk and pick up the list she started. I resist the urge to cross out "steak" and replace it with "stake."

Could I really do any of this? I may very well have to. Lisa's right about the situation changing. After last night, it's clear Michael's done waiting patiently at my window for an invitation, and if I have any hope of getting my life together, I need to take Lisa's advice and deal with him once and for all. My best hope is he'll listen to reason.

Michael, I've been thinking about our relationship, and what with you being undead, and me not being into all that— well, I have to be honest and let you know this inviting-you-in thing is never going to happen. I know, it seems like I've been leading you on all these months, and I kind of have been, but I've realized that the reason I broke up with you before is because we have nothing in common, and you being a vampire has only widened the gap. But just because you're not technically breathing doesn't mean you can't make something of yourself. I'll bet there are plenty of opportunities for the undead in the fast-food industry! Wendy's is always looking for help with the drive-thru window late at night.

Of course, dead or alive, Michael was never the kind of guy to take no for an answer, and maybe "breaking up" with him and pissing him off would be the stupidest plan ever. It'd probably be easier to get close to him if he thinks I'm still all hot and bothered to let him in my window. Get close to him and *do what?* is the question. Stake him? How do you stake someone who says they love you—even if they are already technically dead?

I think about all the times Michael's lost his temper in the last few months—those moments when he said or did something and fear took over my body; how he threatened Lisa. Despite what I said, he's really *not* the same old Michael and I need to concentrate on that.

I shake my head and look out my window at the tree. I follow the branches with my eyes, then focus on the worn bark where he usually sits. At the very least I should be prepared, and what would be more appropriate than a stake made from the damn tree?

I unlatch the window, then push up the pane and screen. I reach out and pull a branch, bending it back and forth until the wood starts to split. Sweat breaks out on my forehead as I yank and twist the branch around, finally pulling it off the tree. I shut the window and wonder how hard it'll be to whittle the tip into a point. Too bad they didn't cover stakes in eighth-grade woodworking class. I look down at my chest. How far do you have to push a stake in before it pierces someone's heart?

So what now? Sharpen the stake in case things get ugly with Michael—the pointier the better? Plan a speech that leaves his ego intact in the hopes of avoiding using said stake?

I go over to my desk and root around in my junk drawer for the pocketknife I got during my one year in Girl Scouts. I spot the large cross my mom bought during her brief church-going binge after the divorce. It's bigger than I remembered, at least thee inches long. I close it in my palm and try to feel its antivamp energy.

Nothing.

I turn it over. Gold plated. Not even solid. I don't remember reading that it has to be made of any certain type of metal, like the bullet for deep-sixing werewolves. God, should I start worrying about werewolves, too?

I roll my eyes and put the chain around my neck, hoping the power of the cross is brought forth by some cosmic otherworldly thing and not by the total time I've spent in church.

I put a check next to the word "cross" on the list Lisa made. I flip the paper over and bite my lip when I see the heart surrounding Danny's name that I'd crossed out last night. I look at his name and think about Rachael's word association. *What's the first word that pops into your head when you think about Michael? About Danny?*

Regret.

I regret that I ever got involved with Michael. I regret that I let things spiral out of control.

I trace the heart with my finger. I regret letting Danny slip through my fingers. And I want to tell him how much I miss him. That I miss the *me* I was when we were together.

I look at my clock. I should get some sleep so I have enough energy to deal with Michael tonight. He's the priority here, right?

No. The priority is getting my act together and taking back my life. Dealing with regret.

But, what would I say? *Hey, Danny, I know you blew me off last night, but can we talk?* I look at my phone and my stomach flutters. I programmed his number in last summer—not that I ever called. I picture Rachael pointing at the phone, saying the *new* me isn't afraid to make a call. Lisa's voice echoes in my head, telling me to deal with my problems head on.

I pick up the phone and scroll down to Danny's number. What's the worst thing that could happen, besides utter humiliation?

I take a deep breath and push the button.

One . . . two . . . three rings.

"Hey, it's me, Jordan. I was wondering if maybe you could, um, come over and talk."

CHAPTER THIRTEEN

I look in the mirror for the hundredth time and hope Rachael was right about Danny liking the natural look. Or in this case the haven't-been-to-bed-yet-and-look-like-hell-warmed-over look.

I head back over to my bed and lightly bounce my index finger on the stake's point as I watch for Danny through the window. I consider e-mailing the Girl Scouts of America to suggest they offer a badge for whittling vampire stakes.

Finally I see Danny jog around the corner and toward the house. I stash the stake in my night table drawer, in case Danny ends up here, because sharp-pointed objects in the bed would definitely be a mood killer.

I shake my head. If I'm going to do this right, Danny won't be coming upstairs today.

The doorbell chimes and my confidence wavers. Just because he agreed to come over doesn't mean things are going to go my way. Hell, he could be planning to drive home the point that there isn't anything between us anymore. I take a deep breath and pray I won't throw up on his feet.

I open the door and look at his flushed cheeks and the nervous smile on his face. "Hi, thanks for coming over."

His smile widens and my shoulders relax. "No problem." I step aside to let him in, but he hesitates. "Are your parents awake?"

"My mom and my stepfather are upstate at a christening; they'll be back later today."

He's gnawing on his lip.

"Is that a problem?"

"Um, I guess not. It's just that my mom doesn't like me hanging out if there aren't any parents around, but she thinks I'm out for a run. I shouldn't stay too long, though."

I lead him into the living room and cringe as he looks around at the flowered wallpaper, flowered couches, and flowered area rug. "Pretty over the top, huh? Like a florist's truck threw up. My mom saw this design in some decorating magazine. It's supposed to make you feel like you're in an English cottage garden, but all the patterns make my head spin."

Danny nods and sits in the recliner—built for

one. He's keeping his distance. I lower myself onto the couch, sinking into the pillows. My confidence is ebbing away.

"Did you do something different to your hair?"

"Rachael did it. She thought I needed a change."

"Oh, it looks nice. Uh, not that it didn't before."

"Thanks."

"So how was the party? I'm kind of surprised you're up so early," he says.

"I haven't been to bed yet."

"Oh, I guess it was really good, then."

"Actually, it was pretty crappy. I stayed up all night making sure Kassie Campbell didn't wrap her car around a tree." And avoiding Michael.

Danny nods again. "Kassie's a trip, huh?"

"Yeah." I will my brain to say something scintillating to move past the small talk. "So your mom doesn't like you hanging out without parents around?" Real brilliant.

"No, she's kind of fanatic about that. Your mom left you alone for the weekend?"

"Yeah, ever since my parents got divorced, dating took priority over parental supervision. Then, after she married my stepfather, who's this huge wine snob, they go winery-hopping all the time. Let's just say I got pretty good at entertaining myself while they travel."

"Your dad is in South Carolina, right?"

"Yeah . . . Not exactly an easy place to get to for the weekend, even with an airline ticket. But we're old enough to take care of ourselves, right?"

"Not according to my parents." He pushes up his sleeve and checks his watch. "So," he says, dragging his teeth across his lower lip, "what did you want to talk about?" He raises his eyebrows expectantly and I just about melt.

"I, uh, wanted to talk about what happened last summer—you know, after Melissa's party. You called me and I never called you back, but it's not because I didn't want to. I kind of have this phone phobia thing. I was hoping you would call again, but . . ."

"I didn't want you to think I was stalking you or anything, and after four unreturned calls I assumed you were hoping I'd get the hint."

"No! I, uh . . ."

Good Lord, I won't be winning any prizes for articulation today.

Deep breath.

I look into his dark gray eyes, and remember how comfortable it always was with him. "I really, really wanted to call you back. A lot of stuff was going on last summer, but the thing I regret the most is not calling you back. And the more time passed, the harder it was to even think about picking up the phone, and I didn't even know if you were still interested, and . . ." And there was this "little problem" with Michael.

A big grin erupts on Danny's face. "So when I said I missed you in class, I wasn't making a total fool of myself?"

I let out a laugh. "No. God, no."

"Good, because I've been kicking myself for that the past few days."

"Can we start over? I'd really like to."

"Yeah, I'd like that, too, but there's some stuff you should know first. Before we're, like, official and everything."

"I'm intrigued, I think." *Please don't tell me you've been experimenting with guys.*

"It's kind of embarrassing, and it's why I couldn't go that party and all."

"I could fill a book with the embarrassing situations I've ended up in in the past few years." *Why, just last night I was half naked in a room full of people, making out with an asshole!*

"Well, two summers ago my brother, Matt, and I were hanging out with Aaron Forbes. Do you remember him?"

"He used to go to our school, right? Little guy."

"Yeah, he goes to Saint Christopher's now. But anyway, Aaron's parents have this pub in their basement, with keg taps and stuff, and we kind of spent the summer, uh, boozing it up."

I shrug. "Okay. You know, been there, done that." *Still doing it.*

"Well, it, uh, turned out to be a big deal. One afternoon his mom found us passed out, and Aaron wouldn't wake up. He had to have his stomach pumped. Not surprisingly, my parents totally lost it—

especially my mom. And Matt and I had to get jobs working for my uncle's landscaping business so we could pay the Forbeses for all the beer we drank and the damage to the pub."

"Okay, you were young and foolish—it happens."

"Yeah, I guess it happens, but not to my mom—not to her babies. She's turned into this militant breath-checking nut. I can't go anywhere without her calling parents. She'd do background checks on the whole town if she could."

"Well, nobody I know has totally normal parents. Lisa Dolan was here this morning, and after she was 'away' her mom is pulling the same stuff."

"I didn't know you and Lisa were friends."

"We were, you know, in elementary school, and part of middle school." I shrug again. "So is that it? You haven't been having a torrid affair with Mademoiselle Chubb or anything?"

He laughs. "Not until she loses the mustache!"

We both laugh, and I think maybe Danny won't judge me too harshly if I ever take a stab at true confessions.

"But seriously, you just need to know that if we get together, it may not be what you're used to. I can't stay out past ten thirty—eleven if she's feeling generous. And my mom will be watching us like a hawk. She'll probably grill your mom about what's going on over here, too."

"Like my mom has a clue."

"Yeah, well . . . also . . . I know you like to go out

and party, but I can't be with you when you do."

"But I don't have to . . ."

"Wait, let me finish." He purses his lips together. "I hear Gabby and Janine talking at play practice and I assume you're doing the same stuff, and that's okay, but until my mom works through *her* stuff, I'm not going to be Mister Exciting." Danny looks down at his lap. "So?"

He looks so cute and worried. I want to run over and hug him. "I think riding to track meets with you last spring was the highlight of my year."

Danny lets out a long sigh. "Oh, so okay, so we're, uh . . ."

I feel this huge, warm smile break out on my face. "Yeah, we are."

Danny gets ups and sits down next to me. He picks up my hand, and I hope he doesn't notice that I'm shaking. "I was scared you were going to blow me off because I can't . . . you know."

I lean in and we kiss. It feels so good. I know I should be enjoying it, I *am* enjoying it, but I can't help thinking about talking to Michael tonight.

Danny pulls back. "I *really* hate to go, but if I don't get home soon my mom will release the bloodhounds."

"It's okay. I *really* should get some sleep, anyway. Hey, can I ask you something?"

"Anything."

"Was it hard when you stopped, you know, going to Aaron's house everyday?"

He's blushing, and I wish I could tell him not to be

embarrassed, that I'm envious he's already tackled the stuff I'm still struggling with.

"Yeah, at first it was. But it was mostly a relief. I mean, it sucked being hungover all the time—and worrying about getting caught. Working with my uncle helped, gave me something to do, kept my mind off of it. Being afraid of my mom helped, too."

I nod. I wish I were like Danny. I wish everything were behind me instead of crouched outside my window, ready to pounce.

He stands up. "I'd better get going; my aunt is throwing this birthday party for my grandmother and I'm supposed to help set up a tent in her backyard. If I don't get home too late, I'll give you a call."

"Great."

He takes my hand as I walk him to the front door. His fingers twist with mine, and shivers run up my arm. I resist the temptation to redirect him to my room. I need to trust that I don't need to ambush him in order to seal the deal.

I open the door and he leans down and kisses me again. "I'm really glad you called me," he whispers in my ear.

I watch him jog down my driveway, then shut the door and sprint up the stairs. "I did it!" I scream, running into my room. "And he kissed me. Yes! Yes! Yes!" I squeal as I throw myself on my bed and hug the pillow to my chest. I can still smell him. I can still smell that wonderful salty sweat smell, the way he smelled on the bus rides back to school after meets. I pull my shirt up over my nose and breathe him in. Oh, so much nicer than that damn coconut crap Michael wears. I can't believe I ever liked that smell—like the cardboard palm tree deodorizer Janine hangs in her car.

I reach over to grab my phone to call Rachael but decide it's too early. At least I *wanted* to call her.

I put the pillow under my head and pull my comforter up to my chin. I should get some sleep—a couple of hours, at least, and then I can figure out what to say to Michael tonight. I yawn and close my eyes, thinking about how perfectly Danny's hand fit with mine.

"Jordan?"

I bolt up in bed. My room is dark and gray. "Mom? What time is it?"

My mother flips on the light. "Three thirtyish. We just got home. Do you feel all right?" She bends over and starts picking up clothes.

3:30! Damn, less than two hours of sunlight left.

"I'm fine. I just went out last night and I, uh, got home pretty late."

"Well, it's about time you went out. I was getting worried about you. You know I was talking to Aunt Cathy yesterday and she thinks maybe you need to talk to someone."

I sit up and shake my head. "I'm fine, Mom. Um, look, I should do some homework, and—"

"Oh!" she gasps, her hands waving in the air. "Your hair, I love it. When did you do it?"

Amazing how easily distracted she is from parental concern.

"I didn't do it, Rachael did. It was her idea."

My mom nods and sits down next to me. "You look absolutely gorgeous!" She reaches out and runs her fingers through my hair. Her eyes are sparkling, and I imagine her next move will involve building some sort of shrine to pay homage to Rachael and Clairol for bringing her the blond daughter she'd always hoped for. "Well, perhaps I underestimated that girl."

"Yeah, you'd be surprised how much you two really have in common."

My mom snorts. "I wouldn't go that far, but maybe there's hope."

"Her hair is purple now."

"Oh, good Lord! Well, at least you finally look like the gorgeous girl I knew you could be!"

God, is she even slightly aware of how horrible that was to say?

"Why do you hate the way I look so much?" There, I said it.

"What?" The eyebrows go up.

"Why didn't you like the way I looked before?"

"I don't know what you're talking about. You've always been beautiful." She gets up and smoothes the pleats of her pants. She's going to leave. I know I should be concentrating on Michael right now, but for once I'm not going to let her get away with trashing me.

"You just said I was *finally* gorgeous, which implies

you thought something about my appearance was lacking."

"That's not what I said."

"Actually it is. And you spend an exorbitant amount of time trying to get me to color my hair, wear makeup, and dress up. Do you even realize that most moms discourage these things? Most moms drill it into their daughters' heads that they look great just the way they are? So I guess I've always wondered what was so wrong with me that I needed to be fixed up so badly?"

"I never meant . . . I . . ."

"And most moms ask about homework, and want to know exactly where their kids are and what they're doing."

"Jordan, really."

"And most moms know if their kids are having problems."

"Look, I don't know where this is coming from, but anything about your appearance I've mentioned was just to help you feel more confident. And I have always trusted you and respected you, and I've never felt the need to be one of those parents who keeps her child on a leash. And most *teenagers* would relish the freedom you enjoy."

"Yeah, I relished getting so trashed last night that I almost slept with a stranger—*again*. I relished driving my friend around last night because she was too drunk and coked up to get behind the wheel. I relish swiping booze from the liquor cabinet and smoking pot with my friends. I am *totally* relishing my freedom, Mom."

I almost smile as the color drains from my mom's face, leaving the pinkish-purple blush across her cheekbones looking like war paint.

"Jordan, I . . ."

"Yes?"

"I-I don't know what to say."

I feel my eyes well up, and I look up at the ceiling, trying to stop my tears. I do *not* want to cry. They tumble down my cheeks anyway, and I clench my fists. God, why am I such a mess? I always thought throwing her poor excuse for parenting in her face would make me feel triumphant and strong. I figured there'd be no way she could justify her behavior, and I imagined her begging me for forgiveness. I imagined shaking my head in disgust because her apologies would just remind me that I am a better person than she is.

But maybe I'm crying because after listening to the list I just spouted off, I don't have a whole lot to lord over anyone.

I'm not better than her—I just have a different set of problems.

My eyes flick over to the clock. I'm running out of daylight. Part of me is relieved, like I've just crossed off another item on my internal list of things to do. Part of me wants to say, okay—catharsis over—I have to move on to the next item: Michael.

My mom sits down on my bed again and sniffs daintily. "What do you want me to do?"

I shrug. "I don't know." Hunt down Michael for me.

"Barbara?" Steve calls from downstairs. "Where's the Verona Pizza menu?"

"Hold on," she calls out. "Do you want to take the day off tomorrow and talk? We can go shopping and do lunch. Figure things out."

"I've been warned that any further absences on my part will result in meetings with Dr. Deluca."

"Barbara? The menu?"

"In a minute!" Her voice is getting shrill. She turns to me. "We can talk now; Steve can wait."

I shake my head. "It's okay. I feel better now that you know. We can talk later."

"You sure this can wait?"

"Yeah."

My mom stands up and pulls a few tissues out of the box on my end table. I think she's going to offer me some, but she walks over to my mirror and blots the makeup collecting in the corner of her eyes. She turns back to me. "Dinner tomorrow? We'll get this figured out." She's smiling—like all my troubles can be fixed in the time it takes to finish a grilled chicken salad and a couple of Diet Cokes.

She pats me on the knee. I wonder why she looks so happy, and then I realize I've just provided her with hours of phone-call fodder to agonize over with her friends. I think I should offer a retraction, but she's already headed down the stairs.

I lie back on my bed. Will I get what Danny has? Extreme parenting? I almost laugh—there's no way Mom is capable of taking it to that level, but I've definitely just thrown away the keys to the free booze-a-rama in the living room. Once Mom fills Steve in, he'll lock everything up—even the cheap stuff.

At least I'll be dealing with Michael sober tonight.

I glance over at the clock again. Time's almost up and I still don't know what I'm going to say to Michael. I open my night table drawer and see *The Vampire Almanac* lying under the stake. I wonder if the author ever imagined her readers would actually need to use any of the techniques listed in the book.

I'd bet she'd wet her pants if Michael came knocking on her window.

I think about what Lisa said; what if somehow Michael made me a vampire? Who would I come back to haunt?

The phone rings.

"Jordan, it's for you," Steve yells.

I lean over, wondering if it's Lisa.

"Hello?"

"Hey, just checking in."

"Hey, Rachael."

"What happened last night? You were supposed to sleep over but then you disappeared. Gabby was all set to leave you, but Janine and I insisted on doing a thorough search. We encountered much craziness, but no you. Some guy did think he'd seen you leave, though."

"Sorry, I went home with Kassie. I tried to find you."

Rachael is laughing. "You willingly spent time with Kassie? Were you totally wasted?"

"Not as bad as Kassie. We kind of drove around until she sobered up."

"Good girl, you stuck to your plan."

"My plan?"

"You know, not getting all trashed. And I heard about blowing off Kyle—and not the way *he* wanted. I think you're showing signs of improvement! And just so you know, I told him you needed to get away from Kassie, but you were on the rebound and not to push anything. "

"I guess he didn't quite get your drift, and I guess I shouldn't tell you I was topless surrounded by empties before I showed signs of improvement."

"All the better! You were sinking and you pulled yourself up. I'm reading this great book about living in the now. You should really read it and—"

"Uh, Rachael?"

"Yeah?"

"I appreciate the call, but it's almost dark, and I have something big I need to take care of."

"Oh. Whatever. Sorry I care."

"No, really I'm glad you called, but it's something big."

"Do I get a hint?"

"I'll tell you about it when it's over."

"Fine."

She's mad. "Actually, there is something I can tell you."

"Yeah?" She's trying to sound bored.

"Danny and I are together."

Rachael is whooping it up, and I'm smiling. I wish I could tell her the rest. Tell her about Michael.

"Oh, my God! When the hell did that happen? Is that the big thing? Come on, spill!"

"It happened around eight thirty this morning, but that's not the thing I have to take care of, that's just a very good thing. I *promise* I'll fill you in on all the details, but for now I really have to go."

"Okay." She sounds sulky, but I can tell she's not mad anymore.

"And Rachael, thanks for calling. It means a lot."

"No problemo. Good luck with your *thing*."

"Thanks." I hang up the phone. "I'll need it."

I sit up in bed and look out my window. The sky is a dark, dull gray. The branches claw at my window as the wind blows by in stiff gusts.

Michael will be here soon to make sure I don't go out tonight. I imagine him waking, stretching stiff, cold limbs. I feel the wind sneak in around the edges of my window, and wonder if the cold air makes him move and think slower. I realize I'm clasping the cross hanging around my neck. It's warm now from resting on my skin. I wonder how Michael is going to take my news. I wonder if Michael's heart is too cold to break.

CHAPTER FOURTEEN

I watch the clock numbers change. 10:48. Where is he? I was so sure he'd be here early tonight.

Skeletal branches wave in the light across the street. I squint into the neighbor's backyard to see if Michael is walking along the fencerow.

I look out at the streetlight again.

Someone is walking down the middle of the road. I laugh at myself for thinking it might be Michael. Michael would never be out walking where anyone could see him. I turn my gaze back to the fences that divide the properties between my street and Lisa's, and realize that, after showing up at Mark's party, I can't be too sure about what he would or wouldn't do. I look out into the street again. The person's getting closer.

I see the light summer jacket Michael was wearing at Mark's party; I see his hair waving in the wind.

I remember how happy I was to see Danny jogging down the street this morning. My stomach flips, and a crop of goose bumps emerge on my arms as I watch Michael coming closer to the house.

He's strutting up the middle of the road, and for a second I think maybe he's always come this way, I just never knew. But I don't really think that's true. I think things are different now.

Michael pauses in the street in front of my house. He looks up and his eyes lock onto mine. His eyes are glowing green, like a cat's in the light, and a nasty smile emerges on his face. He points his fingers like a gun and pretends to shoot me. I flinch and his smile widens.

He jogs down the driveway and leaps into the air. My eyes pop as his body shrinks and transforms in an instant. Heavy wings beat and lift him up toward my room.

Bile rises in my throat as I watch the large bat come closer. The skin stretched taut between the long finger bones catches the moonlight, and I swallow hard. I turn away and lean back against my headboard, hugging my knees to my chest.

Why is he doing this to me? I would *never ever* do this to Danny.

Oh.

Oh, shit!

I get it.

I finally freaking get it!

Michael doesn't love me. If he did, he would have left me alone. He wouldn't have put me through three and a half months of hell.

Michael has probably wanted to kill me since the first day he showed up at my window. I actually have to admire his patience. I never would've thought he had it in him.

I brace myself. I need to get the first word in—take charge and keep the upper hand. I can't let him catch me off guard.

"Boo!" Michael yells as he materializes on the branch closest to my window. I jump, cracking the back of my skull against the headboard.

Round one: Michael.

"Hey, babe! Sorry I'm late, but the craziest thing happened tonight. I was on my way over here and Lisa Dolan showed up! I didn't think I'd made such a great impression last night, what with being pissed to hell you blew me off. But there she was out looking for me and showing the love."

I shake my head. "You're lying!"

"No, seriously, she came looking for me! I don't know why Lisa and I never hooked up when I was . . . you know . . . alive, but there was only so much of me to go around, and short girls never turned me on. But when you've got a live one begging for some action— short or not—how can you say no?"

"Michael, she's—"

"Looking for a fix? I know," he says with a laugh. "Apparently she's been thinking about me all day;

about how I can take her away from the big, bad pain. How I can make her strong again. I told her I'd have to think about it, you know. But we're gonna get together a little later to discuss it further."

He's laughing, and I'm shaking as anger wells up inside me. I hate myself for not figuring out things sooner—for letting things go this far.

"Michael, if there is any part of you that's still human, you'll leave Lisa alone. This is between you and me."

"It still is, Jo. Whatever happens to Lisa will be all your fault. But, frankly, you going out and Lisa showing up was just the kick in the ass I needed. I've wasted three fucking months waiting for you to open this stupid ass window—but I don't need to wait anymore. Tonight's the night, babe. Tonight you'll be *begging* me to come in!"

"I don't want this—I don't want you. I've said it a thousand times, and I will say it again: *I will never let you in!*"

Michael leans in, places his hands on my window, and grins. I see him so clearly now; he looks like the old Michael, except for the sharp teeth.

"Funny, that's not the impression I got on Friday. But don't sweat it, 'cause you're not just going to ask me in tonight, you . . . are . . . going . . . to . . . *beg* . . . me," he says slowly. "I could have had you that first night. I stood by the side of your house and watched you stumble and fall in your driveway. I could have swooped in and torn your throat out, but I'm a patient kind of guy. I knew there'd be a day when you'd beg me to come in, and I knew it would be worth the wait. But enough is enough."

He runs his tongue over his teeth and I suck in my breath, waiting for the windowpane to fog up. I'm praying it'll fog up so I won't have to look at his teeth, so I won't scream. "Jordan, you will beg me to come in," he says again. "You will beg me to come in."

My head feels numb, and I try to resist the urge to call to him.

My lips purse to form the *M* of his name, but I hear a small voice screaming in the back of my head to look away—the fog won't be coming. Michael doesn't breathe anymore, and the window will never fog up. I can't stop looking at his mouth. I can't stop looking at his lips as they form my name.

I don't even hear his words anymore, but I can feel my hand reaching toward the window. The voice is screaming louder, telling me to stop, I sink my teeth into my bottom lip. Blood wells up as the pain snaps me back to sanity.

His eyes lower to my mouth as I lick the blood from my lip. "Oh, Jo, when did you become such a tease?" He leans back. "Cool, though, huh? With very little effort you were about to let me in. You should just give up and get it over with."

"Why are you doing this to me?" Hot tears run down my cheek into my mouth, mixing with the blood.

"Because I love you, Jo," he sings sweetly. "I want us to be together forever." He laughs.

"Why?" Keep it together. Keep it together.

"You really wanna know?"

"Yes!"

"Oh, why the hell not? Lying certainly hasn't gotten me anywhere." Michael leans in and sneers. "The truth is, I've been coming here because out of all the people I knew, you were the weakest and most pathetic, and it's been eating away at my gut that a mess like you had the balls to break up with me."

A laugh escapes from my mouth, but at the same time my stomach recoils like it's been punched. I roll my eyes and shake my head in disbelief. I brace myself to keep my voice from stammering. "You've been stalking me because I broke up with you two summers ago, and *I'm* pathetic?"

"Watch your fucking mouth, or I won't give you a chance to save Lisa." He's not laughing now, and I think it's getting to him that he's still sitting outside in the cold. I need to turn this around.

"Lisa has nothing to do with us. It's me you're mad at, so just—"

"Oh, don't pull any of that psychobabble shit!" he yells.

He leans in again and I see his shoulders relax, but his eyes are wide and wild. I imagine he's trying very hard not to scream at me. "You always thought you were better than me. You read a few books, and you thought you were so much smarter than me. But you know what? I can smell you a mile away. You reek of despair, and I had you. I had you two nights ago and then . . ."

I smile. "And then I got over it. I got over you. I realized I was mooning over a big, fat nothing. I realized that deep down inside, I always knew you were nothing!"

Michael slams his fist into the window and a spiderweb of fractures crack and *ping* through the glass. I figure the only thing keeping the pane together is the same magic that's keeping Michael out.

"I am going to have you, and there is nothing you can do to stop me, Jo."

He's losing it, and I need to at least level the playing field. "Why didn't you fight it, Michael? If you were so damn together, why didn't you fight it?"

"What the hell are you talking about?"

"I think you let that thing kill you. I think you wanted it. There weren't any signs of a struggle. If you didn't have a death wish, why didn't you try to stop it?"

Michael laughs. "You know, you're not so smart. You don't even know when someone's telling you the truth. I didn't lie about what happened. That thing got me and it made sure it looked like I'd done it to myself. Do you really think a creature like that would leave marks so people would come looking for it? You have no idea of the power that's involved. But you will."

"But, I thought—"

"But nothing. I'm not like you. I'm not like Lisa. I

didn't ask for this. I didn't want this. I'm just making the best of it. I loved my life. I loved being king of the world, and that thing ripped it away. Like I'm going to rip yours away, but don't for a minute think I ever wanted this."

So much for common ground.

"Ok, so your life was tragically 'ripped' from you, but why this? Why get so bent about this? We went out for two freaking months."

"Maybe when you're like me—or dead, I really haven't decided—you'll understand. Maybe you'll think about all the meaningless little shits you had to deal with who didn't give you the respect you deserved, all the stupid peons who are still alive and don't even know how to live.

"It's fucking maddening that all these people— people like Rachael, people like *you*—are still walking around, and it's me that's like this."

"What, you were so great you didn't deserve this?"

"That's exactly it! You losers are going nowhere. I was going places. I was gonna be big."

"Yeah, a big freaking asshole."

Michael's mouth drops open, and I wish Rachael were here to see it.

"You know what, I'm out of here. Like I said, I have a lady waiting for me."

"Michael, no—don't go. Let's talk about this."

"Yeah, sorry, but you just bought Lisa a one-way ticket to Vampireville. I was hoping you'd open the window and spare her, but forget it now," he says cheerfully. "Besides, Lisa *really* wants my help with her problem, and I shouldn't let her down. Did you know she couldn't even manage to take enough pills to kill herself properly?

"But it was really fortunate she was here last night, because she knows all sorts of things about you. I guess you should've hid your diary a little better. But the kicker is, after I make her like me, the two of us are going to haunt you. Hell, we may even eat your cat for an appetizer. Then we're going to start picking off your friends—one by one. We'll pay your new buddy, Danny, a visit. Boy, is he going to be sorry he was sniffing around you! Does he know how close you were to letting me in? How do you think he'll feel when I tell him about that before I tear him apart?"

"Michael, stop—don't do this."

"Oh, I'm doing it all right, and the really fun part is we'll keep you alive—for a while—so you can watch it all go down."

He's laughing. I know what I have to say, but the words won't come out.

"Well, babe, I gotta go. Lisa and I are going to work on our suntans before I sink my teeth into that little neck of hers." Michael smiles at me and reaches a hand down to a lower branch.

"No—wait!" I reach under my pillow and slowly wrap my hand around the stake. It's gonna feel so damn good shoving this into his chest. "You can come in—*I invite you in!*"

Michael shakes his head. "Nope. That's not enough. I told you what you have to say."

I hesitate and Michael shrugs. "Okay, I'm off."

"No." I grit my teeth. "I'm *begging* you to come in."

Michael smiles. "That's my girl. I knew you'd do it. I knew you wouldn't let Lisa go down for your screw-ups." He reaches out and my heart feels like it's going to burst as he pushes up the window.

Blood is pounding in my ears. I grip the stake tighter and my legs tense up, ready to move. I have to get him before he gets me.

Michael leans toward the open window. He sticks his head in and rests his elbows on the sill. What is he doing? He props his chin on one hand and purses his lips, as if he's trying to make a decision.

"You know what, Jo? I just don't think this is a good time for me. I mean, as much as I'd really like to come in and get busy on your neck, Lisa is expecting me, and I don't want to disappoint her. I mean, I may be an *asshole*, but she's so *fragile* now, I just couldn't stand her up."

He winks at me. "So, thanks for the invite, but I think it'll be more fun to surprise you some other time. You like surprises, don't you, Jo? Maybe tomorrow. Maybe next week. Just know that I *will* be back. I mean, Lisa and I will be back. And I know Lisa hasn't been *officially* invited in, but seeing as I have, I'll just have to drag you out into the backyard to see her—after

we've ripped your stupid little world apart, that is."
He brings his fingers to his lips and blows me a kiss.
"Later, babe."

Oh my God, no.

"No!" I scream as the stake falls from my hand, and
Michael drops out of sight.

CHAPTER FIFTEEN

Damn it! He had it all planned. He knew I'd invite him
in to save Lisa. He knew it, and now we're both dead.
I hear footsteps running up the stairs. I turn as my
mother throws open my door. Steve pushes in behind
her.

"Jordan, what's the matter?" she shrieks.

Their eyes focus behind me to the open window.

"What the hell is going on?" he asks.

"Uh, a raccoon. It was a raccoon."

"A raccoon?" my mom trills. She takes a step back,
her eyes darting around the room like she's looking for
some rabid fur ball ready to leap out, foam flying.

"Yeah, I, uh, heard this sound and thought it was
Nutty in the tree, trying to get in. But when I opened

the window, it was a raccoon. I, uh, got scared and threw a book, and I guess I hit the window."

Steve rolls his eyes, pushes past me, and slams the window shut. I half expect the glass to shatter apart, but it holds. "Jesus, I'm not paying to heat the neighborhood. You shouldn't be letting that damn cat in that way, anyway." He stands back and looks at the glass. "You're going to pay to get this repaired, young lady, and maybe that'll teach you to think twice before you go off half-cocked next time."

Mom turns to him. "Well, at least it didn't break."

Steve turns to leave, shaking his head and muttering.

"I'll talk to him. Don't worry about this," my mom says, following him out and closing the door.

My head feels like it's going to explode. I sit on my bed and dial Lisa's number with a shaking finger. I'm not even sure what I'm going to say. One ring . . . two . . .

"Jordan?" Mrs. Dolan asks.

"Yes, hi, Mrs. Dolan. I know it's late, but could I talk to Lisa?"

"Lisa went to bed a while ago, but I'll tell her you called."

"Oh, okay, I was just, uh, thinking about her. Do you think maybe you could check on her?"

"I appreciate your concern. Lisa said she told you about what happened, but rest assured, we're keeping a close eye on her."

"But maybe you could check on her, okay?"

Mrs. Dolan exhales. "All right. Good night, Jordan."

"Good night."

I get up and start pacing around my room. Okay, maybe Lisa is asleep, or maybe she's going to sneak out later when everyone else is asleep. Maybe Michael made the whole thing up. What do I do?

The phone rings and I run to my night table. "Hello?"

"It's Mrs. Dolan. Lisa's not in her room, but maybe she's heading to your house again."

Oh, God. "Okay, if she does, or if I hear from her, I'll let you know."

"Thank you. Her father is going out to look for her, but please call me immediately if you see her."

I click the phone off and then back on, and dial.

"Hello?"

"Thank goodness!"

"Jordan?"

"Yeah. I really need your help. Can you get your mom's car and meet me outside?"

"It's kind of late; I was getting ready for bed."

"It's an emergency."

"It's okay that you don't believe me," I tell Rachael. "I know it sounds beyond crazy, but I really appreciate you doing this for me. For Lisa."

Rachael stops the car at a red light and turns to face me. "I believe *you* believe Michael is alive." She glances at the stake sitting in my lap.

"Technically, he's not alive."

"So you said."

"It's true."

"Look, you don't have to prove anything to me. Let's just drive around and see if Lisa is really out and about."

"With Michael."

"With whomever."

I shake the Diet Coke bottle filled with holy water. "I still can't believe you got this."

"God bless bingo, I guess." Rachael laughs. "And, hey, if nothing else comes of tonight, just seeing the faces on those little old ladies when I came charging up the church steps waving the empty bottle around will have been worth it. I think they were so relieved I wasn't after their bingo loot, they'd have done anything I asked."

"You must believe me a little. I mean, you went to all that trouble. Right?"

Rachael shakes her head. "I don't know why I stopped. I looked over at this church, the doors opened and light flooded out. Kind of like it was a sign. I pulled over without even thinking about it. I got something else, too." Rachael reaches over to her purse, her hand fumbling inside. She pulls out a long beaded chain with a crucifix hanging in the middle. "What do you call this? A rosary necklace?"

"Rosary beads." I take it from her hand. "My grandmother had a string of these in every room of her house."

"Some lady just gave it to me. She actually called

after me and put it in my hand. She said she thought I might need it."

"It's purple," I say, squinting down at the beads. "Matches your hair!"

"Fate!" Rachael says. "But I'm not saying I expect to be chatting up Michael Green tonight."

The light turns and Rachael steps on the gas pedal. "So Sea Cliff and Glen Cove were a bust; where to now? Do you want to call Lisa's house and see if they found her?"

"Let's try Bayville first." I slump down in the seat. "I was sure they'd be at Sea Cliff. Michael made some crack about working on his suntan, and Lisa used to live there in the summers."

"Maybe she was afraid you'd come looking for her and figure out where she went. Maybe they're meeting on the tennis courts behind the school. Maybe Michael just said that to throw you off the track."

"No, let's try Bayville."

Rachael yawns and I see her look at the dashboard clock. It's almost one in the morning, and I'm wishing she'd drive faster—Bayville Beach is twenty minutes away.

"Wait! It's too far."

"What's too far?"

"Bayville. Lisa can walk to Sea Cliff Beach, but she'd need to take a car to Bayville, and her parents would hear the engine start up."

Rachael pulls over to the side of the road and puts the car into park. She leans forward and rests her head on the steering wheel. "Jordan, this has been *interesting*, but what do you say we call it a night? Or call the Dolans? It's not like they'd get mad at you for calling so late; they know you're worried. I'll even drive to their house, knock on the door, and ask about Lisa myself."

"No, just drive to the beach before it's too late."

Rachael sighs. "Jordan, I'm tired. We have school tomorrow."

"*Please*, Rachael. Let's check one more time. If they're not there you can have me certified, locked away—anything you want. I just can't let anything happen to her."

"This is so classic." Rachael sits up and turns to me. "Listen carefully: You are *not* responsible for Lisa and how she's dealing with her problems."

"Tell me that again in the morning when we find out Lisa's dead—or worse."

"Listen to yourself. This is crazy. You have to see that this is crazy."

"You didn't hear what he said. If you had, you'd understand."

"Okay, whatever." Rachael puts the car into drive and makes a U-turn on Shore Road. "Let's get this over with."

"Rachael?"

"What?"

"I invited him in."

"What?"

"Michael. I invited him in. I actually tried to let

him in Friday night, but I had to throw up. Tonight I invited him in so he wouldn't go after Lisa."

"So, did he come in?"

"No, he said he thought it would be more fun to come back and do a tag team with Lisa. He can come into my house any time he wants now."

"This is one for the books."

"I wish."

I finger the cross hanging around my neck. Part of me wishes I were crazy. At least Lisa would still be alive in the morning.

The car turns down the big hill to the beach. I strain to see between the houses and trees. We round the last curve and the wind buffets the car. I look out onto the sound. Whitecaps shine in the bright moonlight. My eyes follow the length of the beach.

"Rachael, look! By the jetty." I point toward two figures sitting by the rocks. It's too dark to see their faces from here, but I know it's Lisa's small frame nestled into Michael's.

Rachael turns off the headlights and motor, and coasts into a parking spot. "I see them."

I look at Rachael; her eyes are wide. I grab the stake and reach for the door handle.

Rachael's hand snatches out, her fingers digging into my arm. "Don't go out there."

"I have to!" I pull my arm away and open the door. "I won't let this happen." I get out of the car and a gust of wind blows sand into my mouth. I spit it out as I sprint toward the jetty.

"Jordan, wait!" Rachael yells after me, but I keep running.

The wind is pushing against me, and I wonder if Michael is somehow controlling it—trying to keep me away. "Michael, stop!"

He lifts his head up. A dark smear covers his mouth and chin. Lisa's head hangs limply back, and I'm afraid it will blow off in the wind.

"Leave her alone!" I get closer, and he drops Lisa to the sand and pulls his sleeve across his mouth. Lisa pushes up on one elbow.

"Jordan?" She moves her hand to her neck and then looks down at the blood staining her palm. "Oh, God," she moans.

Without taking my eyes off Michael, I lift the cross over my head and slowly walk toward him.

Michael smiles and licks his lips. "Jo, I thought you'd be cowering in your room. But I guess you missed me too much. Unfortunately, I'm not quite finished here yet, so you'll have to wait your turn." He looks down at Lisa. "Although she may be finished. I'm not sure how much blood she has left. This is the first time I've actually tried out the new choppers on a person, but you know what? One hundred fucking percent better than draining a squirrel!"

"Rachael!" I scream. I take a step closer and raise the stake.

A worried look flashes in his eyes, and he takes a step back. "You gotta be kidding me. You don't actually think you could use that, do you?"

"Without a moment's hesitation."

He steps back again, brushing up against the jetty.

Rachael runs up beside me. "Holy shit," she says slowly, and puts one hand on my arm. "Holy shit."

"Rachael, long time, eh?" Michael says. "Props to you for finally growing some hair. But, babe," Michael smirks, "I gotta subtract points 'cause purple is so not cool."

"Is she okay?" Rachael asks, ignoring him. "Should I call 911?"

"Lisa?" I call out. "You still with us?"

Lisa sits up, her hand pressed against her neck. "Yeah," she says softly. "I'm sorry, Jordan."

I look down at the rosary beads in Rachael's hand. "Do you have the water?"

"Yeah," she yells over the wind. "I can't believe this."

The wind is howling at our backs. My hair is whipping around, stinging my eyes, but I'm afraid to move my hands to brush it aside. I see Michael's eyes dart back and forth from our faces to the crosses. Water splashes over the jetty, spraying us. He looks up at the rock wall. I imagine he could easily jump over it—and just as easily land in the water. Long Island Sound would certainly make a very big bathtub to drown Michael in.

Does he know vampires can't swim?

"Well, ladies, as appealing as a threesome sounds, I think I'll leave you two to Lisa and be on my way."

Michael turns from me to Rachael and takes a step

sideways. Rachael and I lunge toward him, and he slams back into the rocks.

He lets out a nervous laugh. "I guess the cross stuff is true, eh? How about I promise to leave you alone, and we call it even?"

I shake my head. "I don't think so."

Michael purses his lips. "How 'bout you, Rachael? You think that's a good idea? It's pretty cold out here and that coat doesn't look very warm. I can feel the wind blowing right through you. You can't even feel your hands, it's so cold. Rachael, I can feel you shivering. I can feel you turning to ice and letting the cross g—"

"Shut up!" I scream.

I look at Rachael and see her teeth chattering. "Holy shit," she says again.

"I know." I grip the stake tighter. Even without Michael's help, my fingers are turning numb.

"Well," he says, "there's always plan B."

Suddenly Michael shrinks, and a huge brown bat races toward me. "Rachael!"

"I got it!" she yells, flinging the holy water at the bat rising over me.

The wind gusts and I pray some of it will hit the mark. Water ices my skin as it lands on my face and seeps onto my scalp. The bat lets loose a high-pitched shriek and comes crashing down on top of me, knocking me to the sand. "No!" I yell as the cross and stake fly from my hands.

Leathery wings scratch my face, but then it changes,

and Michael is writhing on me, howling. His weight presses down and I can't catch my breath. I hear his skin bubble and crack as my throat silently tries to get some air.

"You bitch!" he bellows, and sharp teeth slash through my coat and into my shoulder. The warm blood is the only thing I feel until Michael's fist smashes my face into the sand.

"Get off her!" Rachael's voice echoes in my ears. I look up and she pushes her cross into Michael's face. He lashes out and knocks her back, then rolls off me, screaming.

My lungs suck in air; hot pain flashes in my shoulder. I scramble on my hands and knees toward Lisa, but he grabs my leg and pulls me back. Knifelike fingernails cut through my jeans into my calf.

"Lisa, help me!" I call out, digging my fingers into the sand to try to pull away from him.

Lisa crawls toward me and reaches for my hand. I scream as Michael's nails cut a trail down my leg.

"Jordan!" Rachael grabs my other hand, and I kick my free leg at his head. He loses his grip and Rachael starts to pull me up, but my leg buckles the second I put weight on it.

Michael yanks my foot back and my hands are ripped from theirs. I land on my stomach, and cold sand grinds into my chin as Michael drags me back.

He heaves me up in his arms and squeezes tight. I can barely breathe, barely move. My ribs feel like they're going to collapse and snap into my chest.

"Get back!" He moves an icy hand up to my neck. "Get back or I'll rip her throat out." He tightens his hold on my neck, and my eyes bulge as a small, wheezing breath escapes my mouth.

Rachael freezes; Lisa falls to her knees, sobbing. "We had a deal. You said you'd leave her alone. You promised me you'd leave her alone."

"Yeah, well, I lied."

"You fucking bastard!" Rachael screams. She starts toward him and flings the bottle of holy water at us.

Only a few drops hit my cheek, but Michael is cursing, so there must have been enough left to hurt him. He drops me and I fall to the sand, gasping for air. My ribs twinge as I turn and look up into his face. A black cross is charred into his cheek at the base of a blistered path that's splattered across his mouth and up over his nose and eyes. In the moonlight, I see sores oozing where curls used to be. He's cradling one clawlike hand burned from the holy water. I think this is how Michael has always looked, underneath it all.

He falls back onto the sand, and I wish the sounds of the waves and the wind were louder than his cries.

Rachael pulls me away from him and hugs me tight.

"Look out!" Lisa yells.

Before I can turn, Michael snatches me away from Rachael, and I'm flying up into the air. My arms and legs wave frantically, trying to find some ground. My right knee smashes into the rocks on the jetty, and I slide across the wet seaweed, toward the waves on the other side. I scrape my hands across the surface, stopping a few feet from the edge. A wave breaks over the rocks, drenching my legs, and I cry out as the salt water soaks through my jeans and into the gashes in my leg.

I hear a thud behind me. "Just you and me now, Jo." Michael pushes his boot into my back, nudging me toward the water. My hands grab at the rocks as I try to find any small crevice to hold onto.

"Rachael, find the stake! Find the stake!"

His foot kicks out again, and I wince in pain as I head closer to the black churning waves. The old pier is only ten feet or so from the jetty, but I don't know if I'd have the strength to swim to it.

His foot jabs into my back again, pushing me closer to the edge. A wave flies up into my face. The water stings my eyes, and I hear him stumble back. My body shakes uncontrollably. Every muscle is cold and sore and battered, but I've come too far to just give up.

"Big man, scared of a little water," I hiss, trembling.

He grabs the collar of my coat and pulls me back from the edge. His cold, blistered face nuzzles my neck and slides under my chin. I breathe in his fetid smell and the sickly sweet coconut stench as his arms tighten around me.

"Stop!" I cry, trying to push out of his arms.

"Do you remember how good it used to be?" he whispers. "How much you loved being with me? I know you miss that. I know you want that again."

His seared lips kiss my neck and I struggle to break

free. "Michael, please." I ignore the pain in my leg and ribs, and try to thrash out of his hold. He squeezes tighter and I cry out.

"Tell me you loved me," he whispers.

"No! Please, no!"

"Tell me." He covers my neck with kisses, and then his teeth pierce my skin. It doesn't hurt like I thought it would; all I can feel are his cold lips clamped down on me. I suddenly feel light, and my eyes roll back as warm blood is sucked away. I hear myself moan as I lean into him. He loosens his hold and I feel myself floating. I feel my blood warming him. All the pain is gone.

"Jordan!" Rachael yells.

I try to call out to her, but nothing comes out. My heart thumps against my chest as Michael's mouth presses harder into my neck.

I hear a crash. Cold water slaps my face and pulls at my body. Michael draws back and another wave crashes across, snapping me out of my stupor.

"Jordan!" I see Rachael slipping on the wet rocks as she tries to make her way over. "I'm coming!"

Michael swears and tries to pull me in again. I can't let him get close to me. I push against his chest as hard as I can. My right leg slips, hot pain shooting up through my calf, but I wedge my left heel between some rocks and shove him away.

"Quick," Rachael says, extending a hand. I reach up for her, but Michael is too fast.

He strikes Rachael across the face "God, you're a pain in my ass!" he snarls.

Rachael stumbles, and I cry out as the stake clatters on the wet rocks. I run my fingers through the seaweed until I feel the point and latch on to it. Michael pulls me up and twists my arm behind my back. "Tell me you loved me," he says, twisting harder. It takes every ounce of energy I have to hold on to the stake.

"Tell me!"

"I never loved you," I say, and he yanks my arm so far back I'm afraid it's going to break.

I slam my free elbow as hard as I can back into his stomach. He releases my arm and I turn toward him, the stake raised high. "I *never* loved you!"

I plunge the stake into his chest, and Michael's mouth forms a shocked *O*—like he can't believe a "meaningless little shit" like me could take him on. He reaches up and touches the wood protruding from his chest. "Jo?"

His eyes meet mine, and I shake my head. "I never loved you, and that is why *I* broke up with *you*!"

I go to push him away, but before I can, Michael Green shatters into a million pieces that catch the wind and blow out across water.

CHAPTER SIXTEEN

It's one of those warm afternoons when you get fooled into thinking winter's over and then the next day some ass-kicking Canadian air blows in and dumps a crapload of snow on top of the bulbs stupid enough to start poking through. But right now with the sun on my cheeks, I can pretend the worst is over.

No, I *know* it's over.

I check my watch. Danny will be here soon and we'll take care of the new number-one item on my list of things to do.

"Any word about when Lisa's getting out of the hospital?" Rachael asks.

I stretch my stiff leg out. "Not yet, but Mrs. Dolan said they're getting her symptoms under control. Oh, did you read in the paper about how she and Mr. Dolan are harassing the animal control people to round up all the stray dogs so no one else has to 'suffer the horror of a wild-dog attack'?"

Rachael laughs and blows her pink-and-blond bangs out of her eyes. I have to admit the color works on her. "I did, and all I can say is, you and Lisa were damn lucky they found some poor mutt near the beach, and it came up rabies-free!"

"Yeah, I wasn't looking forward to a series of shots on top of everything else. But I still think the dog guy knows what really happened—I mean, why else would he have kept the dog under observation instead of putting it to sleep and then testing it?"

"You gotta wonder how many people know what's really out there."

I tap my cane on the front steps. "Hey, you never said how things went last night with that guy from the health food store," I say.

"Marshall was okay, I guess, but—don't be mad."

"What?"

Rachael gives me a guilty smile. "We got pretty wasted."

"Rachael!"

"Hey, I never said I was being good forever—and I wasn't the one getting faced in my room every night."

"I know, but I was dealing with Michael, and, well . . ." I shake my head. "I guess I was doing it regardless. But thanks for sticking with it as long as you did."

Ninety-six days. I've been clean for ninety-six days.

"Well, I don't think I'm going to see Marshall again. He's a little too natural—as in 'deodorant is evil'—natural. Let's just say he was kind of ripe. And not just his pits! Besides," she pauses and blushes, "I think something's starting to cook with Matt."

"Matt? As in Danny's brother, Matt?"

Rachael smacks her lips. "Yup! We've been talking a lot while we've been working on the sets."

"I should've figured something was up. He doesn't usually help out, and you've been overly interested in tagging along when I go to Danny's."

"I wasn't being a tag-along, I was just trying to keep you from being one of those girls who ditches her friends whenever she's hooking up with a guy!"

I tilt my head and smirk. "Like you?"

"I'm reformed."

"Hmmm. Well, seeing as you're Mrs. Douglas's new best friend—"

"Hey," she says, interrupting me. "She needed help with her midlife crisis! At least I've finally found someone who appreciates my advice!" She laughs and blows her bangs aside. "It's actually kind of sad; she can't get enough of the books. She plowed through *My Mother, My Self* in one day, and she was all bummed yesterday when I forgot to bring over *Awakening the Goddess Within*. I ordered a couple of new books, and I'm hoping they'll encourage her to let up on the guys a bit. I mean, it's obvious she's controlling them because her own life is out of control. And if Matt and I hook up, this ten-thirty curfew crap has got to go!"

I nod. "The sooner the better. Going to the early shows and passing people from school in the line to go in while we're on our way home is getting old. Their nights are just starting and Danny's got to drop me off."

"Don't worry, a few more sessions with yours truly and I guarantee Mrs. Douglas will be bending over backward to avoid making her boys into 'adults incapable of making life decisions.'"

"You're kidding, right?"

"Nope, that's what it said on Amazon under *Freedom to Make Mistakes*."

I lean on my cane and stand up. "Let's hope it works." I steady myself on the porch rail and stretch my right leg out behind me. I'd hoped the physical therapy would have done more to get my leg back in shape, but the doctor says I may always have a limp— an eternal reminder of Michael's nails cutting through the muscles in my calf.

"Gabby and Janine were at the movies last night," I say.

"Is Gabby still in the deep freeze?"

"Yeah, when I waved to them she barely acknowledged my existence. At least Janine waved back. She even calls every once in a while to say hello. I can't believe Gabby is being such an asshole about this."

Rachael shakes her head. "I can. She's a classic toxic person. Those kinds of people aren't happy unless everyone around them is miserable. And she's just pissed off because you staying clean is a constant reminder that she's still got a problem. Anyway, it's been a lot easier to digest my lunch without having to listen to her daily binge-and-purge routine."

"Yeah, I don't miss that."

"Plus sitting across the table from Matt is a lot easier on my eyes!"

"Well, let's go out back and make sure the area is clear. Steve will have my head if anything gets wrecked."

We walk around the side of the house to the backyard and Rachael drags some lawn chairs toward the deck.

"How'd you convince them to let you cut it down?"

I look up into the branches and focus on the spot where Michael used to sit. "My mother is terrified of rabid raccoons. I told her they had a nest up there. Plus, Danny said he'd do it for free, and even stack the wood. And it'll make way for this French revival brick patio with built-in grill she's all hot for."

"Do you think it will work?" Rachael asks, plopping into a chair.

"The grill?" I half-hop, half-walk over and sit down next to her.

"No, cutting down the tree. Do you think it will make the nightmares go away?"

In my dream, crashing waves surround the tree. I crawl out my window, and climb through the branches to pull away the old grackle nests. When I lower myself down toward the water, Michael reaches out and sinks his fingers into my leg, dragging me down into the black waves. There's no noise underwater, and when his teeth pierce my neck, I can't hear myself scream.

Goosebumps break out on my arms. "I hope so, but I don't think I'll ever get over being scared of the dark after all this."

"Yeah, the night is definitely a lot scarier now that we know what's out there." Rachael laughs. "My mom is still bugging me about wearing a cross all the time—she totally didn't buy it when I told her it was just a new fashion thing. She's all worried I've secretly converted or something."

Danny's truck pulls up and he honks the horn twice.

I push myself up, cursing as the cane sinks into a muddy spot.

Danny gets out and waves. "Don't get up."

He swings his backpack over his shoulder, reaches into the truck bed, and brings out a black plastic case. "Who needs ear plugs?" he asks, heading toward us.

"Are they used?" Rachael asks.

Danny laughs. "Yeah, but my uncle's ears are more hairy than dirty."

Rachael rolls her eyes. "I'm so glad Matt doesn't have your sense of humor."

Danny puts the chain saw case down and leans over to give me a kiss. It's been three months and his kisses still send a tingle down my spine.

"Is there something going on with Matt that I should know about?" he asks.

"Why, does he talk about me?" Rachael asks, her cheeks flushing.

Danny sits down at the end of my lawn chair and places a hand on my calf, kneading my tight muscles. "Let's just say he seemed disappointed when he got home yesterday and you'd already left."

Rachael claps her hands together. "You know, I have a book for your mother. Maybe I'll bring it by later!"

"Well, be careful. I think my dad's considering placing a bounty on your head for turning my mother on to her self-improvement kick."

"There's always room for improvement, Danny-boy!"

"Yeah, well, he keeps asking her how much all the Pilates and yoga classes are costing him. But she seems to be relaxing a bit, so I'm all for it."

Rachael and I smile at each other. "The liberation of the Douglas boys is at hand," I say.

Danny looks at both of us. "Uh, you know, I'm not even going to ask. But what do you say we get busy and take this bad boy down."

I rub my hands together. "I'm ready!"

"I thought you were going to sit back and let me be manly."

"No, way. This tree is going down and I'm going to do it."

"What about your leg?"

I flex my leg out as far as it will go. I still can't get it totally straight. "How about we do it together?"

Danny raises his eyebrows. "I like that idea."

"Ew!" Rachael stands up. "I think I'll wait inside."

"But I brought you safety glasses," he calls after

her, waving a large plastic set of glasses over his head.

Danny reaches into his backpack and pulls out a small round container and another pair of large plastic goggles. "If you're going to do this, you have to look pretty."

I open the container and slip the two mushy foam pieces into my ears. I strap the goggles around my head and turn to face him.

Danny smirks. "This is a good look on you. It's, uh, very industrial."

I roll my eyes. "Come on."

We walk over to the tree and Danny goes through the process again. I'm not really listening because he's already told me about twenty times. First a cut on the far side of the tree, then one the opposite side. If all goes as planned, the tree falls in the right direction without taking out the back fence.

I gently run my hand on the ax marks he made to show Steve where he was going to make the cuts. Sap is dripping out from the wounds, and for a second I feel guilty for wanting the tree gone. None of what happened was the tree's fault, but I know I need to do this.

"Okay," Danny says. "Any last-minute change of heart?"

I look up into the tree again. Three old grackle nests hang in tatters. "Let's do it!"

"Okay." Danny picks up the chain saw. "It's going to be loud and it's going to shake you up a bit, but I'll be holding it, too. Just let me guide you."

I nod.

Danny starts the chain saw. I put my hands next to his, and we bring it up to the first mark. Pieces of wood fly out and hit my chest and face. My arms rattle as Danny moves the blade deeper and deeper into the tree. It's harder than I thought it would be, and my arms start to ache as the saw cuts into the wood.

"Okay, the other side," Danny yells.

We walk slowly around and lift the saw up higher to the second cut. The noise is deafening, even with the plugs. Danny suddenly turns the saw off, and I see the tree start to move.

"Get back," he says, pulling me into his arms.

An enormous crack echoes out as the tree thunders to the ground, shaking my whole body.

Rachael comes running out and lets out a whoop. She jumps up on the trunk and starts picking her way over branches, toward the top. "You know, I hate to say it, what with me being a tree hugger and all, but that was cool. And the symbolism totally blows me away. I mean, we had this massive thing overpowering us, eating away at us, and we fought back and cut it down, and, well"—she jumps up and down, waving her arms around to keep her balance—"that was just totally cool."

Danny looks at me with raised eyebrows. "Uh, is she talking about the tree?"

I shrug. "You know Rachael, gotta analyze everything." I pull out the earplugs and pop them into their case.

"Uh, right. Well, at least the fence is in one piece,"

Danny says, looking enormously relieved. He turns to me expectantly. "Aren't you going to check out your room? See how it looks? That was the whole point, right?"

"Oh, right. I forgot." I reach down for my cane and wipe off the sawdust.

I head into the house. I hear Rachael singing Little Red Riding Hood's song from the show we're doing. "Mother said straight ahead, not to delay or be misled. I should have heeded her advice, but he seemed so nice."

I'm out of breath by the time I get to my bed. Rachael helped me move it back to the window this morning. I take the large cross I bought off the sill and push the window up.

I stick my head out. The yard feels big and open now. I'm awed by how much space and energy the tree took up.

"I know the leaves aren't out yet or anything, but do you think it worked?" Danny asks.

I nod. "Yeah, it's amazing how much light is coming in through the window now. Amazing."

Here's a sneak peek at
AMANDA MARRONE'S new novel,
REVEALERS

I wake and turn to my window. The witch ball is rattling against the inside of the pane—glowing from a tangled spell within. I wonder which one of my so-called friends threw a hex my way? I watch the spell dance around in the spun glass, and hear the *swoosh* of brooms flying past—capes flapping. One, two, three soft landings rustle the leaves by the back door. The fourth hits the dirt hard, and I smile, thinking Dani better stop scarfing doughnuts or she won't be able to get off the ground much longer.

The ball bursts apart and glass clatters against the baseboard. Margo. Damn her, she's always breaking them. I'll have to ask Mom to make the next one stronger.

I get out of bed and throw on a sweatshirt and jeans. I hope I'll be able to find a hat because it's getting too damn cold flying around on the stupid sticks without one. The last time I suggested we take a car, Zahara practically bit my head off—"We go by air or we don't go at all!" Like she's such the traditionalist. Ha! Wonder what her mother will say when she notices the tongue stud she's sporting.

By the time I get downstairs, they're already walking into the kitchen. I wish my mom would keep the door locked, or put up a do-not-enter spell, if only to keep Margo stewing out in the cold for a few minutes.

Dani waves at me. "Hey, Jules."

Sascha kneels and Nuisance jumps into her arms, nuzzling his chin against her and purring madly.

I scan their faces—only Margo and Zahara seem pissed. Their cheeks are bright red, and I breathe the smoky night air they brought in with them. "Hey, guys."

Zahara clacks her tongue stud on her front teeth. "Nice bed head. Apparently you didn't know we were coming."

I run my fingers through my curls, and look at the cauldron bubbling furiously on the burner— deep-purple steam flying up to the vent. "Mom! Why didn't you wake me up?"

My mom pads into the room and casts a glance at the pot. "Again? Didn't you girls go out a few nights ago?"

Margo rolls her eyes and snorts. "Um, it's not like they run on a schedule or anything."

Mom gives a half smile and shrugs—I hate she's taking that from Margo, but I'm no better. The more Margo and Zahara vie for Queen Bee, the more the rest of us seem to shrink in their wake. Well, not Sascha.

Sascha seems to float outside the circle, only stepping in when things are about to break. But when did this happen to us? When did the need to pull rank get so strong?

Mom sighs as she heads to the stove. "There've been a lot more than usual." She reaches into a jar and tosses some herbs into the water until the steam runs clear. "Do you know who it is?" she asks.

Sascha nods. "Yeah, it's the guy who gutted that Wilkins lady last week. They tracked him down—should be an easy job. Mrs. Keyes said he's at that bar by the river so we should get going before he drinks too much and passes out."

My mom cocks her head and purses her lips. "Sorry I wasn't keeping an eye on it, girls. There's a really good movie on and, well, I guess I was hoping you'd get a few nights off."

Dani flicks her eyes at Margo and Zahara—then flashes a tiny smile at my mom. "It's okay, Mrs. Harris, my mom didn't see it right away, either."

"But she did see it," Margo says. "We didn't have to come fetch you."

"We're all together now," Sascha says quietly. "Let's just go."

"I need to find a hat first." I grab my wool cape from the coatrack and open the closet.

"For God's sake," Zahara says, "it's not that cold!"

I give her a hard look but close the door. "Fine."

Sascha squeezes my hand with icy fingers as we head to the mudroom. "You're going to wish you had a hat—it is *that* cold."

Of course, Sascha wouldn't be caught dead in a hat. She totally gets off on her long black hair swirling behind her as we ride—like anyone is watching. But me, I'll take warmth over vanity, and it's not like a hat could make a dent in my curls.

"Bye, girls," my Mom calls. "Be careful."

I fasten my cape, grab my broom, and follow them out. Sascha was right—it's freaking cold. The wind whips around my face sucking the warm air away. "Just a minute." As I head back into the house—my broom jerks in my hand, ready to fly, and I clutch the smooth handle to keep from losing my grip. I rummage through the bins in the closet and snag my purple hat.

When I get back outside Zahara's jaw is clenched tight—I hear her clacking the tongue stud impatiently on her teeth.

Margo smirks. "That's *real* stylish!"

I pull the wool down over my ears. "Thanks!"

We mount our sticks and Sascha says, "I'll do it." She shakes her long hair so it fans out around her shoulders. "We fly in darkness for the good of all, let us pass unseen till we land again."

A shimmering fog envelops us and we're off. I tip my broom toward the sky and rise up. The frigid air cuts through my cape and I make a note to myself to get my heavy sweaters down from the attic.

Margo flies alongside me. "Your mother needs to get it together. Helena isn't going to tolerate this crap."

"Yeah, well, I wonder what *Helena* would think if she knew you were throwing her first name around like you're best buds? I was under the impression we were to call her Mrs. Keyes. You broke another ball, by the way. What the hell were you trying to do?"

Margo looks down her thin, pointy nose with wide eyes. "It was just a joke—the worst it could've done was give you a good jolt. And as of this weekend I'll be part of the inner circle, and I'm sure Mrs. Keyes will *insist* I use her first name." She grins, points her broom down, and shoots ahead next to Zahara.

I look behind and pull my broom to fall back next to Dani. "Hey," I say. "How's it going?"

Dani shakes her head. "I've got a stupid chem test first period tomorrow. I really should be studying right now."

"Sorry I was late."

"It's okay, but Margo got all bent that we had to come get you. Of course, her mom is always watching their cauldron—always kissing ass."

I laugh, glad to have Dani by my side—on my side.

We ride a ways in silence and then I turn to her. "Things are so weird lately. I don't know what to say or do anymore. I'm always afraid I'll say something wrong and piss Margo or Z off."

Dani nods. "We're supposed to be in this together, but . . ." She shrugs and looks ahead at Margo and Zahara. "My mom said this happened to them, too. She said it always does—I mean, there's only so long five girls can hang without getting on one another's nerves. But we have to try to keep it together. There's no one to take our places yet."

"They're making it harder to want to stay together."

Dani points her chin skyward. "Look at Miss Priss."

Sascha's flying higher than the rest of us—back stick-straight, hair stretching out behind her. "One good gust and she's gonna get blown off riding like that."

Dani draws in closer to me. "Connor's on cleanup tonight."

"I figured," I say, hoping I sound like I don't care.

Dani knows how much I like Connor, though. Of course I'm not the only one who does—there aren't too many cute guys in the coven—especially ones with deep blue eyes. But Connor and I were inseparable until we hit seventh grade and our moms made it clear we needed some distance. I started hanging out with Dani, and Connor spent more time with the guys, but I always wonder if he still thinks about me as much as I think about him.

"Who's helping?" I ask.

She sticks out her tongue. "Michael. Let's hope he put some deodorant on today."

Sascha cuts down in front of us and points toward the parking lot. "There they are."

I nod as we circle the lot and land next to Connor's van. The glamour hiding us blows away as soon as our feet touch the ground. Connor puts the window down. "Hey, what took you so long?"

Margo rolls her eyes. "What do you think? I hope your mom won't be upset."

Connor winks at me and my stomach flips. "Don't worry, Jules, all she cares about is getting the job done. I'll call Michael; he's been buying the guy drinks inside."

I glance at Margo, her frown illuminated by the bar's neon sign, and try not to smile.

Connor punches the button on his cell phone and waits. "Hey! They're here."

"Why don't we head toward the river," I say. As much as I'd love to stay with Connor, I need to concentrate on what we're doing.

Zahara nods and turns toward the sound of the water. "I'll bind him," she says to Margo.

Margo reaches into her cape and pulls out a small bag. "Here ya go." She turns to me as we wind our way through the trees. "Did you finish your *Beowulf* questions?"

"Yeah."

"Can I copy them before class? I was too busy making binders for *Mrs. Keyes*."

"I guess."

Dani tugs on my sleeve and rolls her eyes. I'm pretty sure we're thinking the same thing—Margo's a kiss-ass like her mother.

"Thanks," Margo says. "I forgot how hard it is to roll the stupid things—the damn paper's so thin it kept ripping. It took forever just to get a dozen done."

"It's got to be thin," Dani says, "so it'll break open when you throw it."

"Like I don't know that! I'm just saying they're a pain in the ass to make!"

Sascha puts her hand on Margo's shoulder. "This is a good spot."

We form a semicircle and wait. The river is full and noisy tonight—I hope it'll be enough to mask the sound.

"Here they come," Dani whispers.

"I want you to know I've never done this before," a man's voice says in the dark.

"Me neither," Michael says.

They come around a tree and he sees us.

"What the fu . . ."

"We bind you to the earth!" Zahara yells as she throws the wound paper to the ground at the man's feet. The ball bursts in a shower of blue light. Dirt, sticks, and decaying leaves bind together into snakelike tendrils, wrapping around his feet and twisting up his legs to hold him in place.

I see him cover his round face as I blink away the echoes of light from my eyes. We draw closer to him, our arms stretched out to our sides to form a circle, energy leaping from our fingertips and keeping the circle strong in case he's able to break free.

"What the hell's going on?" he asks, squinting at us. "Mike?"

"I'll go get the bag," Michael says, heading to the van.

"Hey, Mike!" The man struggles to move his feet. "Where are you going? Don't leave me!"

"We hear you're a very naughty boy when the full moon comes out," Margo laughs.

"Let's just get on with it," Sascha says, sounding bored.

"Look, I don't know what you're talking about. I was just coming out here for—"

He pauses, and I wonder what Michael said to get him to come out here. Puffs of breath leave his mouth in short bursts. He pulls at his knees, but the forest floor holds him tight.

"We have reason to believe you're responsible for some recent werewolf activity," Zahara says like she's a cop. "What do you have to say for yourself?"

"Shit," he says. "Look, I've never hurt anyone; I take precautions."

Zahara laughs, and clicks her tongue stud on her teeth. "Funny, I think Annie Wilkins and Steven Gardener would beg to differ—if they were still alive, that is."

"Steven was before I got a watcher. And, and . . . Annie, that was an accident, I swear. I—I liked Annie . . . I never would've hurt her on purpose. Something went wrong, but it'll never happen again."

Margo nods. "Damn straight it'll never happen again."

"Come on," Sascha says. "Let's just do it."

"He needs to show some remorse!" Zahara snaps.

"Oh my God, you're part of that group, aren't you? Oh God, no. I'll leave town, please," he begs. "Just let me go!"

Tears glisten on his cheeks. I hate when Zahara drags it out like this; I hate how I start feeling sorry for them.

Zahara shakes her head. "All right, fine."

The man smiles—he doesn't realize she was talking to Sascha.

We all face our palms toward him and yell, *"Reveal!"*

Yellow light swirls around him, forming a ball above his head. He looks at the sky with wide, terrified eyes. I know he's feeling the change coming, and instinctively searching for the round moon that isn't there.

"What did you do to me? It shouldn't be happening—it's not time!" he screams. "Please, just give me another chance!"

I want to look away but I never do. I need to see the change so I can steel myself for what comes next.

His face twists and expands into a long snout. I'm glad the water crashing behind us drowns the groan of bones growing at a remarkable pace. His clothes tear and drop. I get a glimpse between his legs, and feel my cheeks flush. Dark coarse hair grows, covering him, and he's complete. He snarls at us, jerking his muzzle from one person to the next, swiping the air with razor claws.

I reach into my cape pocket and take out my gun. Arm straight, I aim at his chest and fire. We all step back to avoid the spray as he goes down. I don't watch his body change back—I want to remember him as the wolf and not the man. It makes it easier to sleep at night.

Michael walks past with the body bag. "Nice work."

"Anyone want to hang for a bit?" Connor asks as he helps Michael spread the bag.

Margo smiles. "Love to!"

Zahara lifts a flask from her cape. She takes a swig and hands it to Margo. "Me too—we could head back to your house, Connor. Margo's got a bunch of binders to give your mom."

Connor looks at me. "How about you, Jules?"

I shrug, feeling drained. "I should head home; I'm tired and it's late."

He pouts his lips, and I almost change my mind, but Zahara and Margo exchange looks, and I don't feel like dealing with any more of their crap tonight.

"Hey, Michael, what did you tell the guy to get him out here?" I ask, changing the subject.

Michael looks up and winks at me. "Blow job."

Shaking my head, I take the flask from Margo. The cool metal stings my lips as the brandy burns its way down my throat. I hate the way it tastes, but Zahara refuses to fill the flask with wine or anything else because "brandy is the traditional afterkill drink." Of course, it doesn't help having Connor's mother, Helena, in charge of making sure things are ridiculously old school.

I hand the flask to Dani, who takes a quick sip. "I've got a chem test."

Sascha holds out her hand and takes it next. "I've got a French translation to finish." She takes a long drink and puts the flask in her cape. "You don't mind if I borrow this, do you, Z? My mom noticed some of her booze was missing, and she cast some spell on all the bottles so they'll only open for her! But I'm going to need a little buzz to help me get through *Le Petite Prince. C'est tres difficile pour moi!*"

"Okay," Zahara says, "but don't drink the whole thing—I don't want Mrs. Keyes on my ass for going through her good brandy too quickly!"

Sascha pats the flask in her cape and smiles. "I won't." She mounts her broom and heads up through the trees. "Later."

Michael and Connor grunt as they roll the man into the bag.

"What was his name?" I ask.

Michael wipes his sleeve across his forehead. "Uh, Jack."

Connor zips the bag up and stands, wiping his hands against his jeans.

I look up at the sharp crescent moon. "Rest in peace, Jack."

Connor laughs. "You're such a softy, Jules! You sure you can't hang with us?"

"If she's tired, she's tired," Margo says.

Dani sighs. I wonder if she's waiting for Connor to ask her to come over too. She crosses her arms over her stomach. "Well, like I said, I've got to study." She leans in and kisses everyone on the cheek, something we used to do all the time—now it looks awkward and forced.

"I'll go with you," I say, air-kissing Margo and Zahara. I squeeze Michael's shoulder, and then I put one hand on Connor's cheek and give him a long, wet, full-on-the-mouth kiss. He presses my lips with his and I pull away.

"Bye," I whisper. I mount my broom—my heart pounding louder than the water on the rocks. I look at Zahara and Margo and try very hard not to smile at their wide-eyed faces. "Have fun, guys."

As we clear the parking lot, Dani bursts out laughing. "Oh my God, Jules—you so rule! I can't believe you did that. Did you see their faces? Did you? And he totally kissed you back!"

I allow the smile to come now and wonder if he can taste brandy on his lips. I just hope there won't be hell to pay tomorrow.

ABOUT THE AUTHOR

Amanda Marrone grew up on Long Island, where she spent her time reading, drawing, watching insects, and suffering from an overactive imagination. She earned a BA in Education at SUNY Cortland and taught fifth and sixth grade in New Hampshire. She now lives in Connecticut with her husband, Joe, and their two kids. *Uninvited* is her first novel.